Once again she found them standing too close, facing each other in what felt like a void of time, of space. She knew she should say good-night and move away, but she was frozen in place, unable to speak, unable to move. His close proximity to her made her feel trapped, unable to escape even if she'd wanted to.

Her heart thundered as he took a step closer to her. "I've wanted to do this since the moment I saw you."

Before she could draw a breath or prepare in any way for what she knew was about to happen, his mouth covered hers in a fiery kiss that was directly at odds with the dispassionate man she'd thought him to be.

He tasted of sweetened tea and hot desire, and she opened her mouth to him as his arms wrapped around her and pulled her close.

A little voice inside her head told her this shouldn't be happening, but it was happening and it was wonderful.

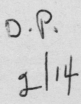
D. P.

2/14

SCENE OF THE CRIME: RETURN TO BACHELOR MOON

Carla Cassidy

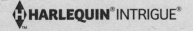

Recycling programs
for this product may
not exist in your area.

ISBN-13: 978-0-373-69727-4

SCENE OF THE CRIME: RETURN TO BACHELOR MOON

Copyright © 2013 by Carla Bracale

Printed in U.S.A.

ABOUT THE AUTHOR

Carla Cassidy is an award-winning author who has written more than fifty novels for Harlequin. In 1995, she won Best Silhouette Romance from *RT Book Reviews* for *Anything for Danny.* In 1998, she also won a Career Achievement Award for Best Innovative Series from *RT Book Reviews.*

Carla believes the only thing better than curling up with a good book to read is sitting down at the computer with a good story to write. She's looking forward to writing many more books and bringing hours of pleasure to readers.

Books by Carla Cassidy

*The Recovery Men

CAST OF CHARACTERS

Marlena Meyers—She never dreamed she'd be at the center of not one but two crimes and fighting a desire for a man she knows is wrong for her on every level.

Gabriel Blankenship—FBI profiler sent to Bachelor Moon to discover the mystery of the disappearance of the entire Connelly family. He's a lone wolf, damaged by life yet drawn to Marlena, who might be the key to solving the crime.

Pamela Winters—A maid at the bed-and-breakfast who took an instant dislike to Marlena when she returned to Bachelor Moon and made a valued place for herself with the family who owned the B and B.

John Jeffries—The gardener at the bed-and-breakfast and a man willing to go to any lengths to hide his secrets.

Thomas Brady—A local carpenter who has a romantic interest in Marlena. Has he decided if he can't have her then nobody will?

Brian Walker—The ex-mayor of Bachelor Moon. His daughter, Samantha Walker, was murdered by a man obsessed with Daniella Connelly. Is he looking for payback?

Ryan Sherman—An ex-con who's had several run-ins with Sam Connelly. Has Ryan's explosive temper caused him to harm Sam, his wife and child?

Chapter One

"Tell me again what we're doing checking out the whereabouts of an ex-FBI agent from the Kansas City field office?" FBI agent Andrew Barkin asked from the backseat of the car.

FBI special agent Gabriel Blankenship slowed the car as they approached the city limits of the small town of Bachelor Moon, Louisiana. "We're doing this as a professional courtesy, because the Kansas City office asked us to."

"A little over two years ago Sam Connelly was a respected FBI profiler before he came out here for a two-week vacation and fell in love with Daniella Butler, who owns the Bachelor Moon Bed-and-Breakfast," Jackson Revannaugh drawled from the passenger seat. "Apparently true love won out over career climbing. Sam quit the agency, moved here and he and Daniella got married."

"Sam not only became a husband but also stepfather to Daniella's daughter, Macy. And this morning we received a call from the manager of the bed-and-breakfast that all three of them are missing," Gabriel said.

"Unusual that we'd be sent out, since it hasn't even been twenty-four hours," Jackson observed.

"According to the manager, they've been missing since last night." Gabriel kept his gaze focused on the road ahead, knowing that the bed-and-breakfast was ten miles outside of the small town.

His gut feeling was that this was all a wild goose chase, some sort of misunderstanding between the manager and the family she worked for. It was an hour and a half drive from their field office in Baton Rouge, and they hadn't been dispatched to leave until past three that afternoon.

Hopefully they could get this sorted out and he would be in his own bed, back in his comfortable ranch house in Baton Rouge, before midnight.

He'd been surprised when Director Jason Miller had assigned two men to travel with him to check out this supposed disappearance, yet he had been grateful for the company of the men, who were not only good agents adept at processing crime scenes and sniffing out bad guys but were friends, as well.

"There." Andrew pointed ahead to a sign that indicated to turn right for the Bachelor Moon Bed-and-Breakfast.

Gabriel made the turn, squinting against the bright hot sun. He drove on for three more miles and then turned again, following another sign leading into a lane that took them to their destination.

"Nice," Jackson said as a huge two-story house with a sweeping veranda surrounded by large trees came into view. On one side of the B and B, a big pond glittered in the overhead sun, and on the other side, a giant carriage house looked inviting with large pots of multi-colored flowers along its perimeter.

The employees must park in another area, and there must be no guests, Gabriel thought, for the parking lot in front of the house was empty. He pulled the car to a halt and shut off the engine. At the same time, the front door opened and a woman stepped out on the porch.

With the sun sparkling off her short, curly blond hair, creating a halo effect, she looked like a slender angel. Her long bare legs exposed by a pair of white shorts and her shoulders by a pink tank top, she looked like a very hot angel.

"Sweet," Jackson muttered from the backseat.

"On the job, not on the prowl," Gabriel reminded his fellow agent, who had a reputation around the office as a ladies' man. Still, he was shocked by the quick, visceral warmth that swept through him at the sight of her. Her eyes had to be blue, he thought.

She started down the steps as if unable to wait for them to join her on the porch. As she drew closer, the men exited the vehicle.

Two things occurred at the same time: Gabriel flashed his official identification and noted that her eyes weren't blue, as he'd expected, but rather an electric green. She was more than pretty with her slender face, wide eyes, straight nose and generous mouth, but at the moment all of her features were radiating an emotion somewhere between panic and unadulterated fear.

"Thank God you're here," she said after Gabriel had introduced himself and his two men. "I'm Marlena Meyers, the manager here, and I'm the one who sounded the alarm this morning. I called the sheriff first, but he was afraid to get involved in what might be federal business, so he said I should contact the FBI. I found Sam's contact list in his bedroom and called his former director with the Kansas City field office."

"And Assistant Director Forbes contacted our field office in Baton Rouge and here we are," Gabriel replied. Despite the fact that the sun was slowly sinking in the west, the mid-July heat and humidity made it difficult to breathe. "Can we go inside?"

"Oh, of course." She whirled on the heels of her white sandals to lead them back to the house. Gabriel couldn't help but notice the shapeliness of her butt in the tight shorts as she walked ahead of him—and that irritated him.

It had been a long time since a woman had attracted his attention in any way, and the last thing he needed was to be distracted by this blonde bombshell. He just wanted to get inside, figure things out and get back home as soon as possible.

She led them into a great room, obviously a place decorated for guests to hang out. Besides a couple of couches and chairs, there was a flat-screen television and a bookcase full of paperbacks and puzzles.

She paused in the center of the room, and her gaze shot from Andrew to Jackson and then finally landed on Gabriel. "They're gone." Her voice was a tortured whisper as her eyes became shiny with unshed tears. "When I got up this morning, I knew that something was horribly wrong."

"And how did you know that?" Gabriel asked.

Her eyes darkened, and she twisted her ringless hands together. "You need to see the kitchen." Once again she turned and walked out of the room. The three men exchanged curious glances and followed.

"This is the guest dining room," she said as they entered a room with a table big enough to seat a dozen. A sideboard held an industrial-size coffee brewer, but no scent of coffee lingered in the air.

She paused at the door on the opposite side of the room, her eyes still shiny. "There," she said and pointed into the room. It was obvious she had no intention of going inside.

As Gabriel swept past her, he caught a whiff of her scent, a clean floral fragrance he found instantly appealing, but the allure of her perfume immediately died as he walked into the kitchen and saw the table before him.

The small round wooden table on the far side of the roomy kitchen held the remnants of what appeared to be an evening snack. Three glasses of milk sat next to three small plates with cookies. Milk was missing from all of the glasses, and there was one cookie on one plate and two each on the other plates. A single chair was overturned on its back on the floor, as if the person seated in it had jumped up so quickly that it had flipped over.

"The back door looks like it's unlocked," Jackson said.

None of the three men had taken more than two steps into the room. "Has anyone been inside here besides you?"

She shook her head, her blond curls dancing with the movement. "No. We don't have any guests right now, and I've made sure the other help have stayed out of the kitchen all day."

Gabriel frowned. "Before we do anything more here, I'd like to see their bedrooms."

"They live in the two-bedroom suite upstairs."

"Are they the type of people to take an impromptu trip somewhere?" Gabriel asked as they all followed her up the wide staircase.

"Not at all. If they had planned anything, they would have let me know, and they would have never taken off in the middle of the night." Her voice was laced with a simmering frantic worry. "Something bad happened last night. I just know it. Now they're gone, and nobody has seen or heard from them all day."

Gabriel had known the moment he had stepped into the kitchen that he wasn't going to make it into his own bed tonight. Although his gut told him they'd just looked at a crime scene, he didn't have enough information to fully embrace that as a certainty.

Upstairs there were guest rooms on either side of the hall. Gabriel paused at each doorway to look inside. The first was decorated in blue and white and held two double beds, a dresser, a small table and chairs next to the window.

The second held a king-size bed and was a study in lavender and lace, with the same type of furniture again. There appeared to be nothing amiss in either of the rooms.

"The guest rooms have their own baths, and there are three more rooms in the carriage house," she said, flipping on lights, even though night wouldn't encroach for a couple of hours yet.

"Where does this go?" Gabriel asked, referring to a closed door in the hallway.

"It leads to an old servant's staircase that goes down to the basement and outside. Nobody uses it anymore, and the door is kept locked."

Gabriel nodded, knowing before the night was over that the door would be unlocked and the basement thoroughly checked.

"These are Sam, Daniella and Macy's rooms." The door was already open, and Marlena paused in the hallway and gestured the men in.

The initial space was a large bedroom/sitting area. The king-size bed was neatly made with a black-and-white spread. At the foot of the bed was a settee in front of a wall-mounted flat-screen television. A set of bookshelves held games and books, and it was easy for Gabriel to recognize that this was the family getaway from a houseful of paying guests.

The bathroom was also neat and clean, with no indication that anyone had been there during the day. The smaller bedroom was an explosion of pink with a single bed covered with stuffed animals and dolls.

Gabriel returned to the main room and opened the closet doors as Jackson and Andrew checked the bathroom and Macy's bedroom more carefully.

Gabriel noted a set of suitcases were shoved to the left of the closet, and there didn't appear to be any clothing missing from hangers. He moved to the dresser, where two phones resided side by side. He couldn't imagine the Connellys leaving without taking their cells with them. He picked up the phones and noticed that both were turned off, probably shut down for the night before their owners had gone to bed.

He then pulled out the top drawer of the dresser, dismayed to find Sam's wallet and his gun. A check in the wallet let Gabriel know that his driver's license, credit cards and bank card were all intact.

Gabriel's heart stepped up its rhythm as he tried to imagine any reason a man would take off with his family without his wallet. And an FBI agent would never leave for any extended time without his gun. It just wouldn't happen.

He turned to see Marlena still standing in the hallway. "You'd better set us up with rooms for a night or two. It looks like we're going to be here a while. And don't allow anyone into the kitchen. Right now that appears to be a crime scene."

One hand shot to her mouth in obvious horror. "You have to find them."

Gabriel nodded. "That's the plan, and the first thing I need to do is ask you some questions." Marlena Meyers might be pretty, and she appeared genuinely distraught, but he had to figure out if she was truly scared for the people who had been her bosses or a good actress who was somehow responsible for whatever had happened in that kitchen the night before.

Of the three FBI agents, Gabriel Blankenship intimidated Marlena the most. Since the moment he'd met her, his blue eyes had remained dark and flat, his lips seemingly unable to curve into any semblance of a smile.

Within minutes it was established that agents Barkin and Revannaugh would share the blue room and Gabriel would take the lavender room. While the other two men went out to their car to bring in duffel bags and crime-scene kits, Gabriel gestured her into a chair in the common room downstairs and then pulled up one of the other chairs close enough so that their knees practically touched.

Marlena wanted to scream at him that he was wasting precious time, that he and his men should be out checking the woods, beating the bushes, knocking on doors in an attempt to find the missing family.... Her surrogate family.

From the pocket of the white shirt that stretched across impossibly broad shoulders, he pulled out a pen and a small pad. He was definitely a hunk, his black slacks fitting perfectly to his slender waist and long legs. He also wore a shoulder holster and gun that would constantly remind her he wasn't a guest here but rather a man on a mission.

His black hair had just enough curl to entice a woman to run her fingers through it, but those eyes of his would stop any impulse a woman might have to touch him in any way.

Cold and with a glint of keen intelligence, his ice-blue eyes appeared to be those of a man who had seen too much, who trusted nobody and held not a hint of any kind of invitation.

"How long have you worked here as a manager?" he asked.

"For the past seventeen months or so. Before that I was living in Chicago, although I'm originally from Bachelor Moon. Daniella and I were best friends all through high school. I left here around the time she married Johnny Butler, and when I returned, I found out Johnny had been murdered and she had fallen in love with Sam." She knew she was rambling, giving him far more information than he'd asked for, but it was nerves. Whenever she was nervous and frightened, she talked too much.

"I was maid of honor at Sam and Daniella's wedding, and for almost the past two years, the two of them and little Macy have been my family." New tears burned at her eyes but she quickly blinked them away. "They took me and Cory in when we had nothing and no place else to go. They embraced us, and my friendship with Daniella picked up where it had left off."

He stared at her mouth, and she wondered if he was somehow judging the words that fell out of it. Did he believe she'd had something to do with the family's disappearance? Did he think she was lying to cover up some sort of heinous crime?

He turned his attention to the pad in his hand, made a couple of notes and then gazed up at her again. "Cory?"

"My brother. He just turned twenty, and he works as the gardener's assistant here. My mother abandoned us when we were young, and my father... Well, he did the best he could, but I basically raised Cory. When I was twenty my father died, and I petitioned the courts to get custody of Cory, and he's been with me ever since." Again she realized she was talking too much and firmly chastised herself just to answer his questions as simply, as succinctly as possible.

"And where does Cory stay?"

"He has a small apartment built onto the back of the carriage house, but he'd never do anything to hurt Sam or Daniella, and he thinks of Macy as a little sister. He loves them as much as I do."

"Who else works here?"

How she wished he'd just give her a hint of a smile, a tiny indication that he understood the panic that seared through her soul, that the fabric of her fragile world had come undone and she felt utterly lost.

She frowned and focused on his question. "The housekeeper is Pamela Winters. She lives in an apartment in town and only works two or three days a week, depending on the guest load. Then there's John Jeffries. He's the gardener and lives in a cottage down by the pond. John's the only person who works here full-time besides me and Cory."

"What about other part-time workers?"

She was aware of agents Barkin and Revannaugh returning to the kitchen, where she knew they'd be looking for further evidence to substantiate the possibility of foul play.

"Daniella does most of the cooking for the guests, but she occasionally has Marion Wells come in to take over the job for her. When we're really busy, Valerie King comes in to help with the cleaning. But none of these people would have any reason to do anything bad to Sam and Daniella. We all love them, and Macy is the smartest, cutest little girl on the face of the earth."

A sob caught in her throat and she quickly choked it down. "You shouldn't be wasting your time sitting here and questioning me. You should be out there someplace looking for them," she said passionately.

His blue eyes stared at her dispassionately, and she decided at that moment that she didn't particularly like Special Agent Gabriel Blankenship. "I assume you live here on the premises. Where is your room?"

"Just off the kitchen." She caught her lower lip to keep it from trembling.

He raised a dark eyebrow. "And when was the last time you heard or saw the family?"

"Last night around eight. They went upstairs and I went into my rooms."

"I'd like to see your rooms." He stood and looked at her expectantly.

She felt as if he viewed her as a suspect, and she didn't like the feeling. She stood, her feet leaden as she thought about going through the kitchen to get to her rooms, the kitchen where she knew something bad had happened to people she loved.

She was acutely aware of him following behind her as she passed through the kitchen, where the two agents were fingerprinting the back door. They nodded to her as she went to the door that led to the suite of small rooms she had called home for almost two years. There was a sitting room, a bathroom and two small bedrooms, one where she slept, and one that she and Daniella had turned into a storage room.

The sitting room was relatively plain—a sofa, a rocking chair and a television. There were no knick-knacks or trinkets to mark the space as hers. She'd traveled light through life, with her brother the only thing of importance to her.

Gabriel stepped into the room, and it instantly

seemed to shrink in size. She became aware of his scent, a faint but pleasant woodsy cologne.

His blue eyes narrowed and a frown furrowed his brow as he took in the immediate surroundings. He glanced into the storage room and then stood in her bedroom doorway, his back a broad mountain in front of her.

Thank goodness there were no silk panties sneaking over the top of an open drawer, no lacy bra hanging from a doorknob. Marlena was definitely grateful at the moment that she was a neat freak.

He whirled around to gaze at her speculatively. "You were asleep right here, and you didn't hear anything in the kitchen that caused you concern last night?" His deep voice was rife with disbelief.

"I get up at the crack of dawn, work hard during the day and I sleep hard at night. I've always been a deep, heavy sleeper, and unless somebody screamed, I probably wouldn't have awakened." She raised her chin a notch.

"So you don't think anyone screamed."

She hesitated a moment and then shook her head. "I can't be positive, but I'm relatively sure that a scream would have pulled me from my sleep."

He held her gaze, and she fought the impulse to squirm. It was as if his piercing blue eyes attempted to crawl inside her head, look into her soul, and she realized at that moment that she was his number-one suspect in whatever had happened to the family she loved.

Chapter Two

Gabriel woke at dawn, smothered in lavender sheets and a bedspread, pulled from an erotic dream involving himself and his number-one suspect.

Not a good way to start a new day, he thought as he got out of bed and padded into the adjoining bathroom. Minutes later he stood beneath a needle-hot shower spray, trying to burn out the memory of his unusually hot dream.

Marlena Meyer's long silky legs had been entangled with his as they'd kissed and caressed each other. Her green eyes had glowed with a hunger that had made him want to satisfy her. Thankfully he had awakened at that moment.

It had been a short night of sleep. He'd insisted Marlena get her brother and John, the gardener, last night and get them to the house to be interviewed.

The interviews had lasted for several hours, and after a search of the basement and all other areas of the house, it had been around three o'clock in the morning when Gabriel had finally crawled into bed.

Andrew and Jackson had finished processing the kitchen. They'd found hundreds of fingerprints, probably mostly those of the family and the staff. Interestingly enough, the door and frame had apparently been wiped clean, as not a single print had been found there.

There was no question in his mind that the family had not gone willingly with whomever had walked through that back door. The real question was why had they been taken, and how had somebody managed to corral three people and take them away without Marlena in the next room hearing anything?

Other than the overturned chair, there were no signs of a struggle, no indication that anything violent had occurred in the kitchen.

Thank God he and his men had packed bags to be gone for a couple of days, for he had a feeling this wasn't going to be an easy one to solve.

Although his gut told him the Connelly family was either in deep trouble or already dead; the evidence didn't automatically point to a crime taking place. All they had at the moment was circumstantial evidence that something had happened to the family.

He needed to check the financial records, both the personal ones for the Connellys and those of the bed-and-breakfast. Although unusual, the Connelly family wouldn't be the first one to just up and walk away from their current life, leaving behind not only hundreds of questions but loved ones without any sense of closure.

The one thing that bothered Gabriel about this scenario was that he couldn't imagine a former FBI agent walking away without his gun.

Gabriel stepped out of the shower, dried off and dressed in a fresh pair of slacks and another white shirt, and by that time he thought he smelled the faint scent of coffee drifting upstairs.

He checked his watch. It was just after six. Apparently Marlena had been telling him the truth when she'd told him she was up at the crack of dawn.

As he walked down the stairs toward the dining room, his thoughts were scattered on all the things that needed to be done in order to further investigate the disappearance. He carried his laptop, deciding that he'd work from the dining room rather than upstairs in the lavender room.

They had released the kitchen back to Marlena late last night, after they were sure that it had been checked from top to bottom for evidence. Photos had been taken, along with measurements and drawings, notes and impressions.

The coffee smell came from the dining room, and he spied the full pot on the sideboard, along with cups and saucers and all the accoutrements that anyone might need to doctor up a cup of java.

He placed his laptop on the table that had been set with plates and silverware for three and then bypassed the room and entered the kitchen, where Marlena stood with her back to him at the window. Apparently she didn't hear him, and for a moment he said nothing to draw her attention as memories of his inappropriate dream drifted through his brain.

Again today she was dressed in a pair of shorts, denim ones that hugged her pert, shapely butt and showcased the length of her long legs.... Legs that he'd dreamed had been wrapped around his. An apple-green T-shirt topped the shorts, and he knew the color would make her eyes pop.

She turned suddenly, and a startled gasp escaped her. "I didn't know you were there."

"I just got here," he replied.

"I've got biscuits in the oven and gravy ready to make." She took several steps away from the window, and her gaze fell on the table. "I want to thank your agents for cleaning up in here."

"The plates and glasses were bagged and tagged. All they cleaned up was the mess they'd made in fingerprinting."

"Still, I appreciate it." Her eyes were dark, as if in genuine pain as her gaze remained focused on the table. She finally glanced back at him. "There's coffee in the dining room, and you just let me know when you want breakfast, or if you want something besides biscuits and gravy, and I'll be glad to serve you in there."

He nodded. "Biscuits and gravy sounds good, and after we eat, I'd like you to take me on a tour of the grounds."

Her eyes widened in surprise, but she nodded her assent. "I'll have breakfast ready in about fifteen minutes." She turned toward the stove as if to dismiss him.

He hesitated a moment and then returned to the dining room, where he helped himself to a cup of coffee and opened his laptop to begin work.

He hadn't seen a personal laptop in their suite. The only computer had been in the small office off the great room that was obviously used for the business.

Heavy footsteps let him know Jackson approached. Jackson was a slender man, but he walked as if he weighed ten thousand pounds. Gabriel offered the dark-haired agent a tight smile as he entered the dining room.

"Ah, coffee… The drink of gods," Jackson said as he headed for the sideboard.

He poured himself a cup and then joined Gabriel at the table. "So, looks like a potential abduction to me."

"That's what I'm thinking," Gabriel replied. "I've already let Director Miller know how things stand here. I'm in the process of getting a financial picture for both their personal life and this business. After breakfast I'm walking the grounds with Marlena, and I want you and Andrew to search for a personal computer or laptop, plus get into the one in the office, and see if there's been any unusual activity that might yield clues as to what happened here."

Jackson nodded and Gabriel continued. "I also plan on bringing in the part-time helpers sometime this afternoon to interview them, and later I'd like you and Andrew to head into town and start asking questions."

"Breakfast first, and then work," Andrew said as he ambled into the room and headed toward the coffee.

"Of course, breakfast first," Jackson said with a grin. It was office intrigue about what Andrew loved most: his job, his girlfriend or food. There was a rumor that he'd once eaten his weight in meat and desserts at a local buffet in Baton Rouge.

Andrew joined them at the table, and for the next few minutes the men spoke about the interviews they'd conducted the night before with the gardener, John Jeffries, and Marlena's brother, Cory.

John Jeffries was thirty years old, originally from New Orleans, and his alibi for the night of the disappearance was that Cory had been at his cabin and the two of them had been watching horror films and had fallen asleep. According to both Cory and John, they'd slept through the night, John on the sofa and Cory in a recliner, and had both awakened around seven the next morning.

They all stopped talking when Marlena walked in carrying a huge basket of biscuits, a small tray of butter and a variety of jellies. "I'll be right back with the gravy," she said, looking at none of them as she set the basket and tray in the center of the table between where the three sat.

"And what are our thoughts of the lovely manager?" Jackson asked in a low voice.

"The verdict is still out," Gabriel replied. What he'd like to know is if her hair was as soft, if her lips were as hot as they'd been in his dream. He frowned, shoving away these unwanted thoughts. "As far as I'm concerned right now, she's at the top of our suspect list. If nothing else, she's a person of interest who might know something that will solve this disappearance."

He slammed his mouth shut as she returned to the room, carrying a large bowl and ladle of sausage-scented gravy.

"Mmm, smells good," Andrew said, having already opened a couple of the biscuits on his plate.

For the first time Marlena smiled, and the sight of it shot unwanted warmth through Gabriel's stomach.

"I hope it tastes as good as it smells," she replied, and then once again left them alone.

What was wrong with him? Why was this woman already under his skin? Gabriel grabbed one of the warm biscuits and tore it open, irritated by the unfamiliar feelings Marlena Meyers evoked in him.

Although Gabriel had enjoyed sex with a number of women over the years, it hadn't been that often, and it had always been just sex, with the understanding that he wasn't a *forever* kind of man. There was no place for love in his life, never had been, never would be.

Still, something about Marlena Meyers made him think of hot sex, of tangling his hands in her impish blond curls, of feeling the spill of her naked breasts in his hands. It had been a very long time since any woman had affected him this way.

Get a grip, he told himself irritably. She was at the very least a tool to use to gain information on a potential crime, and at the most, potentially responsible for the disappearance of the Connelly family. Not a woman to fantasize about, not a woman to get close to in any way.

All he wanted from her was answers, and to that end, once the meal was over and he knew he'd given her enough time to clean up the kitchen, he went in search of her to accompany him for a walk around the grounds.

It had been too late last night to fully view the surrounding area, and it was possible that some clue or bit of evidence might be found outside.

If the family were being held alive someplace on the property, then before dusk fell, Gabriel would find them. If the family was dead and their bodies were still on the property, then they'd be found as well, before the end of the night.

It was just after eight-thirty when he and Marlena

left by the front door, the heat and humidity already like a slap in the face as they walked outside.

"I thought it was humid in Baton Rouge, but this makes Baton Rouge feel positively arid," he said as they stepped off the porch.

"That's why July and August are our slowest months of the year. We only had two couples booked for the next few weeks, and I emailed them this morning to cancel their visit."

"Hopefully we can tie things up here before the next couple of weeks," Gabriel replied. He pointed toward a shed near a dock that extended out over the pond. "What's that?"

"It's a bait shack. You don't think…" Her voice trailed off as if her thought was too horrible to say out loud.

"I need to check it out," he said grimly.

"I'll wait here." Her voice trembled as he left her side and walked onto the planks at the front of the dock. The bait shop was an oversize shed, and the door was closed.

From outside the wooden structure, he could hear the faint hum of something electric, probably a refrigerator and tanks to hold live bait. He pulled from his pocket a thin latex glove and then reached out for the doorknob, his heart taking on an unsteady rhythm.

Were Sam and Daniella and little seven-year-old Macy dead, their bodies shoved inside this small building? Although Gabriel had worked difficult cases in the past, it never got any easier to work a case where a small child was involved.

He grabbed the doorknob, drew in a deep breath

and then opened it. A whoosh of relief escaped him as he saw exactly what he'd hoped to see: a refrigerator, several wells holding minnows, a screened-in box full of live crickets and no bodies.

He looked back at Marlena and shook his head. Even from this distance, he could see the relief that washed over her pretty face. He met her on a graveled path that led near the edge of the water.

"Does the pond have big fish?" he asked as they fell in step together.

"Some of the guests have pulled out real beauties," she replied. "Mostly catfish and bass and the ever-present bottom-feeding carp."

"Do you fish?"

"No way. This is as close as I ever get to the pond or any body of water bigger than a bathtub." Her eyes darkened with a hint of fear. "I never learned how to swim."

He absorbed this information as he did every minute detail about her and his surroundings. "What other buildings are on the property?" he asked, focusing back on the reason they were taking this walk.

"Just a big gardening shed, John's place and the carriage house," she replied.

"We'll check out the gardening shed, and then I want you to let me into the carriage house. It was too late last night to search there by the time we processed the kitchen and interviewed you, your brother and John, but we need to check the place and make sure nothing is out of order there."

"Okay," she replied, her voice filled with anxiety.

They walked in silence for a few minutes, following

the path that edged the side of the pond. "You think I'm guilty of something, don't you?" she said, finally breaking the tense silence between them.

She was definitely guilty of stirring an unexpected, unwanted fire of desire inside him. He was aware that she was waiting for his answer. He shrugged. The truth was that, at this moment, he had no definitive answer for her as to whether he believed her guilty of having something to do with the Connellys' disappearance or not.

A WEARY EXHAUSTION battled with the pound of a headache as Marlena cut up fruit to make a salad for the evening meal. After she and Gabriel had walked the grounds earlier that day, Gabriel had spent the rest of the morning on his laptop, while Jackson had worked at the bed-and-breakfast computer in the tiny office just off the common room. Andrew had gone into town to ask questions and make arrangements for Marion Wells, Valerie King and Pamela Winters to come to the house to be interviewed.

Around noon Marlena had placed a platter of ham and cheese sandwiches, along with a big bowl of potato salad, on the table. She had stacked the plates and silverware, allowing the men to eat whenever they were ready rather than calling them to a sit-down meal.

All the rules had changed. From the moment she'd awakened and found the family gone, the neat and orderly world inside the bed-and-breakfast had been shattered.

Marlena was on the verge of shattering every time she thought of the missing people she loved. Daniella had been like a sister, and in the past two years, Sam had become like a favorite brother-in-law. Seven-year-old Macy was the icing on the cake in the family Marlena had temporarily claimed as her own.

Marlena had spent most of the afternoon either in her room or in the kitchen preparing dinner. She'd decided to serve the men a hearty meal of smothered pork chops, mashed potatoes and corn. The fruit salad would be perfect to finish off as dessert. She knew that Gabriel had spent the afternoon interviewing Marion Wells, Valerie King and Pamela Winters, but she suspected those women knew no more than she did about what had happened.

The back door creaked open and she jumped, nearly slicing her finger. She relaxed as she saw her brother step into the kitchen. Lately, most of the time she wanted to take him by the shoulders and shake some adult sense into him, but at the moment, the sight of him was a welcome one, and her heart filled with love.

"Hey, sis. How's it going?"

"It's going," she replied.

He slumped into one of the chairs at the table. "This is all so weird."

"Scary weird," she agreed, and then couldn't help herself. "I thought you were going to get a haircut last week."

He raked a hand through his shaggy blond hair. "I didn't get around to it yet, and don't start nagging."

She grinned ruefully. "I don't have the heart or the energy at the moment to nag you. How about a glass of chocolate milk? You know chocolate milk solves everything."

A hint of a smile curved his lips, and she knew he was thinking of all the bad times they'd gone through in the past. Chocolate milk had always been her panacea. "That sounds good," he agreed.

She made the milk with chocolate syrup, stirred it until it was foamy and then set a glass for Cory and a glass for herself on the table.

"Thanks." He took a drink and then looked at her. "I saw you walking with that detective this morning. Is he giving you a hard time?"

"Gabriel Blankenship. And, no, he isn't giving me a hard time, but he's doing his job. By the end of our walk this morning, my head was spinning from all the questions he'd asked."

"Questions like what? Surely he doesn't think you had anything to do with this."

She took a sip from her glass. As always, the sight of Cory caused love to well up inside her. He had the face of a choirboy, open and earnest, with blue-green eyes that radiated a soulful innocence.

"I don't know what exactly he thinks about me, but he asked me the questions I would expect under the circumstances. Did Sam and Daniella have any enemies? Had either of them been threatened recently? Had their moods changed in the past few days? Of course, my answer was no to all of them."

"How did this happen? Do you think whoever took them will come back to take us?" His eyes simmered more blue than green.

"Oh, Cory, I don't think so. I don't think any of us are in danger." But she wasn't sure if she believed the reassuring words or not.

Without knowing who had taken the Connelly family and why, without knowing exactly what had happened in the kitchen the night they disappeared, there was no way to know if there was still danger lurking about or not.

"Are you eating with the others in the dining room tonight?" she asked. Cory often sat with the guests for dinner.

"Nah. John and I are heading into town for pizza."

"It's nice that you and John get along so well." She finished her milk, placed the glass in the sink and then returned to slicing up the last of the fruit.

"He's cool. He's kind of like a father, always telling me how to do things and teaching me stuff. We caught two rattlesnakes today, cut off their heads and threw them into the woods."

Marlena's heart filled with sorrow for her brother, who had lost his mother and father far too soon. Although Marlena had done everything in her power to fill Cory's needs and see to his care, she knew she hadn't been a substitute for a masculine presence in his life.

"As far as I'm concerned, the only good snake is a dead snake," she replied. "I'm glad you have John. Every boy needs a male role model in his life, but don't forget our future game plan."

"Yeah, yeah, I remember." He finished his milk and stood. "I'd better get out of here. We have some work to do outside before we head into town for dinner." He walked over to her and kissed her on the temple. "You sure you're okay?" he asked in a surprising role reversal.

"I'm hanging in there," she replied, a surge of pride fluttering in her heart as she realized the child she'd raised was showing all the signs of becoming a man.

By the time she placed dinner on the table, the house was empty except for herself and the three agents. She served them and then returned to the kitchen, where she ate her dinner at the table where Sam, Daniella and Macy had been interrupted in a nighttime snack.

Their absence was a physical pain in her heart, and she knew it would be there until she got some answers. Hopefully Gabriel and his men had come up with something during the day's investigation.... A clue, a potential motive, something that would find the family alive and well.

After the men had eaten and she'd cleared their dishes and cleaned the kitchen, she retired to her private rooms, figuring the best thing she could do was stay out of the way of anything the FBI agents were doing to investigate.

It was after eight when a knock fell on her door. She got up from the rocking chair and opened the door to see Gabriel.

"May I come in?" he asked.

Surprised, she opened the door farther and motioned him to the sofa, then sank back in the old wooden rocking chair that squeaked faintly with every rock. "Did you find out anything today?" she asked, trying to ignore the pleasant woodsy scent that had followed him into the room.

"Several things, but nothing concrete to provide a trail to follow." As usual, his handsome features appeared set in stone, and there was no warmth, no welcome at all in the depths of his eyes. "I stopped in to tell you that it isn't necessary for you to cook for us. We aren't paying guests here, so we aren't your responsibility."

"I really don't mind, and besides, it keeps me busy. I'll go crazy with nothing to do around here," she protested.

He leaned against the sofa back, seeming to shrink the size of the piece of furniture—and the entire room—with his presence. "Pamela Winters is not a fan of yours."

Marlena couldn't help the short burst of laughter that escaped her at his understatement. "Pamela Winters hates my guts."

"Why is that?"

Marlena rocked several times, the squeak of the chair the only noise in the room as she thought of the dark-haired woman who worked as the head housekeeper.

Marlena finally stopped her movement and focused on the man asking the questions. "I think Pamela thought she was going to become the manager once Daniella decided to give up some of the reins of the daily running of the place. Unfortunately, when I arrived here, penniless and with no place else to go, Daniella not only took me under her wing, but she instantly appointed me manager. I don't blame Pamela for feeling betrayed, but somehow her anger has been pointed at me. We're civil with each other, but she's made it clear she doesn't want to be my friend."

"She thinks maybe you had something to do with

the disappearances because you might be named a beneficiary in Sam's and Daniella's wills."

Marlena gasped, and then laughed again. "That's ridiculous." Her laughter died, and she began to rock back and forth with a sense of both outrage and fear. "First of all, I refuse to believe that they're dead, and I'll repeat again, I had absolutely nothing to do with their disappearance. Second, they would have never made me a beneficiary. Daniella knew this was just a stopping place for me and Cory, that it was temporary until we gathered our resources to get on with our lives, and that we were planning on leaving soon."

"Get on with your lives? What does that mean?"

She was aware of the piercing quality of his eyes and the simmer of some indefinable energy between them. "My goal was never to be a manager of a bed-and-breakfast. Cory and I are planning to eventually move to a bigger city where I can get a teaching degree, and he can get some sort of technical training. I want the house and the dog, the husband and the children. Daniella and Sam knew that this job was just temporary for me, that I had different dreams than staying here in Bachelor Moon. Are you married?"

"No, and have no intention of joining the ranks of the married set. I like living alone. I wouldn't do marriage well, so there's no point in trying it." He stood suddenly. "I'll let you get back to whatever you were doing before I came in."

She got out of the rocking chair and followed him to the door. "Actually, I'm thinking of taking a little walk. I could use some fresh air."

"Then I'll just say good night." Gabriel gave her a

curt nod and left, heading back through the kitchen and dining room toward the stairs to his room.

Marlena left her room and stepped through the kitchen door that led outside. She breathed deeply of the humid, floral-scented air. Darkness had fallen, but a full moon shone overhead, easily lighting the path that led around the pond.

Her head ached with all the questions, the fears, the utter horror of the past twenty-four hours. What had happened to Sam and Daniella and Macy? It was as if an alien spaceship had shot down a beam that had instantly drawn them up and out of the house, leaving no identifying clues behind.

She couldn't imagine who might want to hurt the Connellys. They were respected, warm and giving to both their guests and the community of Bachelor Moon. Daniella served on a half dozen charity committees, and Sam was the man people called on when they were in trouble or needed something done. Macy was everyone's delight with her sassy attitude and sweet, loving heart.

As she neared the area where the walkway came closest to the pond, a chorus of bullfrogs sang a deep-throated tune and a faint splash indicated that the fish were jumping.

It was a beautiful night, and yet all was wrong with the world. Tears burned at her eyes as she thought of the people she loved, people who were missing without any apparent reason.

The path she followed stopped abruptly at the far end of the pond. A trail led off to John's little cabin but a sign indicated that guests weren't allowed on the narrow path.

She turned and started back the way she had come. Her thoughts shifted to the man in charge of the case: Gabriel Blankenship.

She was both drawn to and repelled by him at the same time. His intensity nearly stole her breath away. Something about him made her pulse pound a little harder, her heart race a little faster. She recognized it as some sort of strange attraction, but he was certainly the last man she'd want any kind of relationship with.

He was here to do a job, and when the job was done, he would be gone. He'd just told her that he wasn't the marrying type, and marriage was definitely on her wish list. She'd thought that was where she was headed with Gary Holzman when she'd lived in Chicago, but that dream had exploded and she'd wound up here with nothing but a beat-up car spewing fumes, a suitcase full of clothes and Cory.

She'd just about reached the part of the walkway that was closest to the pond's edge when the sound of rustling in the brush behind her stopped the bullfrog's song.

She had no chance to turn, no time to process that danger was coming before she was shoved from behind with enough force that she flew forward and was weightless for an instant—airborne—and then she plunged into the pond.

Headfirst she went down...down, with no idea how to get up.

Chapter Three

Although it was relatively early, after the short night before, Gabriel had told both Jackson and Andrew to head to bed and get a good night's sleep, as he intended to do himself. He was certain the next day would be a long one, and he wanted them all to start out rested.

He stripped down to a pair of boxers and then opened the window, despite the air-conditioning that kept the room cool and pleasant. Since the age of seven, Gabriel had always kept his bedroom window open, never knowing when he might need to make a hasty escape from a raging drunken father.

Certainly more than once throughout his childhood, he'd used the window to flee the wrath of George Blankenship. Like Marlena's, Gabriel's mother had abandoned him and his father when Gabriel had been seven. She'd left him in the hands of a brutal man who'd either beaten him half to death for unclear reasons or ignored him until Gabriel was old enough to exit and never look back.

He'd lived on the streets, worked a hundred different jobs, and waffled between a life of crime and a life of investigating crimes. He'd finally managed to make his way through college with a criminal justice degree and a minor in psychology, and that's when the FBI had brought him in as a profiler.

He loved his job and he was good at it, but this particular case already had him frustrated by the lack of leads. The bank records had shown no red flags either in the personal or business finances. The email accounts showed no threats or unusual activity. So far he and his team hadn't spoken to anybody who didn't admire or like the family.

Granted, they were still in the beginning stages of the investigation, but he knew that, in many disappearances, within the first couple of hours, the taken were killed.

What he didn't know yet was who had been the intended target. Was it Sam, and his wife and step-daughter were merely collateral damage? Was there something in Daniella's past that might have brought this on?

He turned off the light in his room and got beneath the lavender top sheet, his mind whirling a million miles an hour. There had to have been more than one person involved; otherwise how was it possible for a single individual to neutralize three people and get them out of their home? And Marlena had heard nothing, which meant either she was lying or whoever had come in and taken the three people had done so relatively silently. How was that possible with a seven-year-old little girl in the mix?

The sound of a splash came from outside the window—a loud splash. Must be a fish the size of a minitorpedo, he thought. A thrashing noise followed, and then a faint cry.

Definitely a female cry. Marlena had told him she was going out to get some fresh air. Who had made that splash? Had it been a fish, or her?

Gabriel bolted up from the bed and flew out of his room. He stumbled down the stairs two at a time, his heart surging with adrenaline as he remembered she couldn't swim.

As he flew through the lower level of the house and into the kitchen, he noted that Marlena's door to her rooms was open, as was the back door.

He burst out into the hot night air and again heard a splashing and a frantic cry from the pond. By the time he reached a vantage point where he could see the water, the moon glittered down on the smooth surface.

He frowned. Had he only imagined the cries? Had he fallen asleep in bed and not realized it, dreaming that Marlena, who couldn't swim, was somewhere in the pond?

As he stared at the water, it bubbled and rippled and then Marlena's pale face broke the surface. Panic etched her features as she managed a single cry before sinking beneath the surface once again.

He raced to a place where he could dive from the short wooden dock into the pond. He hit the water, grateful that it was as warm as a bath, and swam quickly to the place where he had seen Marlena go down.

Diving underwater and opening his eyes, he realized the murky water made it impossible for him to see anything. So he used his hands and legs to search for her, hoping he wasn't already too late.

How long had she been in the water? He surfaced,

drew a deep breath and then went under a second time, his heart pounding frantically.

He swam all around the area where he'd last seen her, his arms outstretched before him. Where was she? Had she already succumbed to the water?

Sharp relief soared through him as he managed to snag an arm. The relief was short-lived as she grabbed hold and frantically wrapped around him like a leech, sinking them both deeper into the water.

Her arms clung around his neck, and in her panic he knew that, if he didn't break her hold on him in some way, they would both drown.

He fought with her, fought for both of their lives and finally managed to wrangle her around the neck and pull her up. They broke the surface of the water, gasping for air, and she immediately tried to crawl onto him to escape a watery grave.

"Marlena." He spewed her name along with a mouthful of water. "You need to calm down. I've got you. Just relax and let me get us to shore."

Still she clung to him, attempting to climb his body with hers as her eyes glowed the iridescent green of a wild animal in the moonlight.

"Marlena!" He managed to dog paddle and grab her by the shoulders, thankful that he was a strong swimmer and a much bigger man.

"Relax, I've got you." He spoke the words slowly and breathed a sigh of relief as he managed to roll her over onto her back. With his arm under her chin, he kept her face well above the water and moved her toward the shore.

Once there, they collapsed side by side on their

backs in the dewy grass, drawing in deep gasps of air. By the time he caught his breath, he realized she was crying and shivering, obviously chilled despite the warmth of the night air that surrounded them.

He got to his feet and pulled her up. "Come on. Let's get you inside and dry."

She continued to weep and shiver as he slung an arm around her shoulder and led her inside. He walked her through the back door to her private quarters and into her bathroom. Spying a stack of towels neatly folded in an open cabinet, he grabbed one for himself and then turned to where she stood as if shell-shocked.

"Marlena, get out of those wet clothes, and then we'll talk," he said. He grabbed a second towel and forced it into her hands and tried not to notice that the wet blouse clung to her like a second skin, emphasizing her breasts and taut nipples.

He turned and left the bathroom, grateful that his boxers were navy and not white. He dried off, wrapped the towel around his waist and sat on the edge of the sofa, waiting for her to emerge from the bathroom.

He needed to find out how a woman who told him she couldn't swim, who obviously had a healthy respect for the water, had wound up in it, nearly drowning.

Had she somehow slipped and fallen into the water? Misstepped in the darkness and wound up sliding down into the pond? There was no question in his mind that if his window hadn't been open, if he hadn't heard the splash and her faint cry, she would have drowned.

After several long minutes, she came out of the bathroom clad in a long pink robe and using a towel to work the last of the dampness from her hair.

Gabriel was shocked by his visceral reaction to her. She looked stunning, and he was grateful for the heavy drape of the towel over his lap, for his body had reacted automatically to the sight of her.

Thank goodness the drama hadn't drawn anyone else's attention. If one of his partners were to walk in right now, the situation definitely looked compromising, as if he and Marlena had taken a tumble into her bed and then showered off afterward.

She walked to the rocking chair and sank down. Dropping the towel she'd used on her hair onto the floor next to her, she looked at Gabriel. Her eyes began to fill with tears. "I would have died if you hadn't been there. You all would have found me floating in the pond in the morning."

The tears that had shimmered and threatened on her long eyelashes fulfilled their promise, and she hid her face in her hands as she rocked back and forth and cried in earnest.

Obviously it had been a traumatic experience for her, Gabriel thought and wondered if he should just leave her alone to deal with the aftermath.

She looked like a woman who needed to be held, who needed to be assured that everything was okay, but he remained firmly seated on the sofa, unwilling to be that man for her.

He told himself it was simple curiosity and nothing else that kept him here in her room after the drama was over. He wanted to know how she'd wound up in the pond.

Finally her tears ebbed, and with a final swipe of her cheeks, she dropped her hands to her lap. "How did you know? How did you know I was in the pond and needed help?"

"I had my bedroom window cracked open and heard a splash and then a faint cry."

"Thank God you heard me." She shivered as if, despite her long robe, there was a core of icy coldness inside her that prevented her from getting warm. "I don't think I could have made it another minute if you hadn't appeared when you did."

"What happened? How did you wind up in the pond?" Gabriel asked, and was suddenly aware of his own bare chest and legs as her gaze swept the length of him, and then quickly moved up to meet and hold his stare.

"I was walking on the path, trying to clear my head. I reached the end and was on my way back when somebody came out of the brush and pushed me hard enough to throw me into the pond." She shivered, more violently this time, as if the full implication of what had just happened to her had been suddenly realized.

Gabriel sat up straighter on the sofa, a thrum of adrenaline rushing through him. "Somebody pushed you? Are you sure it wasn't some sort of animal or something? Did you see who did it?"

"Do I think a crazed raccoon or a big bear suddenly rushed out and pushed me?" She shook her head, as if his question was ridiculous. "It was definitely an animal of the human kind. I felt his hands on my back, and, no, I have no idea who it was. It all happened so fast."

Her eyes darkened and enlarged. "Somebody tried

to kill me, Gabriel. Somebody shoved me off the path and into the water and knew that I would drown."

Gabriel's heart sank. Was she right? Had this been a potential murder attempt, or had it been some sort of weird mistake? Was this somehow tied to the mysterious disappearance of the Connelly family, or was it something completely unrelated?

Time would hopefully answer all those questions. He withheld a deep sigh as he knew this merely complicated what was already a complicated enough situation.

WATER, WATER EVERYWHERE and not a breath to take. Marlena shot up in bed, gasping for the air she hadn't been able to draw in the nightmare she'd just suffered.

A glance at her bedside clock let her know she'd overslept by half an hour, having forgotten to set her alarm the night before.

Gabriel had stayed in her room until she'd finally calmed down. He'd asked several questions about her brush with a watery death, trying to jog her mind into remembering any sound, any scent she might have sensed from the person who had pushed her off the walkway. But she remembered nothing—only the shock and horror of hitting the water and sinking.

What she did remember this morning was how utterly hot Gabriel had looked wrapped in a towel. His broad chest had been sprinkled with just enough black hair to be interesting, and his taut abs had been more than amazing to look at.

But what was really important here was that somebody had tried to kill her last night…or had he?

There was no question that something had bumped

or pushed her into the pond, but had it simply been a figment of her imagination or some sort of mistake, and whoever was responsible had run away, afraid of what he'd accidentally done?

Maybe it had been one of the drifters who occasionally showed up at the bed-and-breakfast looking for a free handout of money or food. Or maybe a local fisherman who had planned to secretly fish in the private pond and had been startled by her presence.

She finally got out of bed, and after a quick shower, refused to dwell on the horror of the night before. In the light of day, she decided that it was probably just some weird circumstance, and she'd been the victim of a sort of hit-and-run accident.

She couldn't imagine anyone wanting to intentionally harm her, but she also didn't plan on taking any more nightly walks alone.

When she left her rooms, she smelled fresh coffee. She entered the dining room to find Andrew seated at the table, a cup of coffee and a plate of leftover biscuits from the morning before in front of him.

"Hope you don't mind that I helped myself," he said.

"Not at all," she replied as she poured herself a cup of coffee and joined him at the table. "Sorry I overslept."

"Not a problem," he replied easily.

She and Andrew had only been talking for a few minutes when Gabriel and Jackson joined them. "Can I get you something to eat?" she asked, half rising from her chair.

Gabriel motioned her down. "Sit and enjoy your coffee. We're heading into town this morning to have a talk with Sheriff Thompson. When I spoke to him yesterday on the phone, I told him I wanted to get the lay of the land here before contacting him face-to-face."

"Jim's a decent man, and maybe he knows something I don't know about Sam and Daniella," she replied.

"Maybe, although he hasn't shared anything useful with us yet. I got the feeling when I spoke to him yesterday that he's still hoping this is a voluntary disappearance and not a crime," Gabriel said.

Marlena shook her head. "There's no way Sam and Daniella would let the people who love them worry about them for this length of time." A new rivulet of fear swept through her for her friends. The only way they wouldn't contact anyone was if they couldn't.

"We have their cell phones in our possession and will be checking any calls that come in, and also looking at those they received before they went missing. Are you going to be okay today with us gone?" Gabriel asked as the other two agents headed for the front door.

She frowned. Last night felt like a nightmare, and even in the light of day a shiver tried to take possession of her, but she shrugged it off. "I should be fine. I'll lock the house and just let in the people I know and trust."

"Have you thought further about anyone who might want to cause you harm?"

He'd asked the same question the night before. "I can't imagine," she said, giving him the same answer. "Maybe I just freaked out a drifter who was hanging around and he accidentally shoved me as he ran away." It sounded lame, but it was the only rational explanation she'd managed to come up with. "Whatever happened, I'm sure it was an accident and whoever was responsible was afraid of getting into trouble."

"Why don't I give you my cell phone number, so if anything comes up, you can call, and we can get right back here?" he suggested.

She smiled at him gratefully. "Thanks. Just let me get a piece of paper to write it down." She hurried into the kitchen, grabbed a notepad then returned to the dining room and wrote down the cell number he gave her.

"We should be back by dinnertime," he said as she walked with him to the door. His gaze held hers for a long moment. "Don't hesitate to call if you need me… us."

As she watched him head to the car where the other two agents awaited him, she decided that maybe Gabriel Blankenship wasn't so bad after all.

She locked the door behind him. Despite what had happened the night before, she felt no real danger directed specifically at her. Still, better to be safe than sorry.

She was back in the kitchen when Cory knocked on the door, eyeing her quizzically through the glass pane. She hurried over and unlocked it to allow him and John to enter.

"Why the locked door?" Cory asked as he sat at the table in the kitchen. John sat next to him. Most mornings the two of them showed up for breakfast, but it was usually Daniella who did the cooking and serving.

"I had a little unexpected encounter with the pond last night." She explained what had happened, and both men looked at her in stunned surprise.

"Thank God one of those agents managed to get to you," Cory exclaimed.

"I didn't know you couldn't swim," John added. "Do you have any idea who might have pushed you?"

"Not a clue," she replied, not wanting to think about how close she'd come to death. "I imagine you two are looking for something to eat. Why don't I whip up a quick batch of pancakes?"

"Sounds good to me," John replied.

As she got out the ingredients to make the pancakes, the three of them talked about the pizza place where the guys had gone the night before, the weeding that needed to be done and the continuing mystery of the Connellys' disappearance.

Marlena liked John. The dark-haired man had an easygoing temperament and had bonded instantly with the younger Cory and kept him busy working by his side on the grounds.

After the two had finished their breakfast, they left by the back door, and Marlena relocked it after them. For the remainder of the morning, she busied herself upstairs, making beds and freshening the rooms where the agents were sleeping.

She immediately knew that Gabriel had slept in the lavender room. As she plumped his pillows and straightened the spread, she smelled his cologne and was surprised by the tiny ray of heat that fired up inside her.

There was no question that she was physically drawn to him, and there was also no question that she had no intention of following through on that attraction. The most important thing right now was that he stay focused on finding Sam, Daniella and Macy.

When she'd finished upstairs, she returned to the kitchen to start a large roast cooking for dinner that evening. An hour or so before mealtime, she'd add in potatoes and carrots.

During the slow months of July and August, Pamela was scheduled to clean two days a week, Mondays and Wednesdays. Since it was Saturday, Marlena would take care of the daily duties to keep the place in shape. Even though Daniella was gone and there were no guests, Daniella would want the routine of maintaining the bed-and-breakfast to continue.

Marlena sank down at the kitchen table with a cup of coffee, her heart crying out for answers. Where were the Connellys? Nobody would ever make her believe that they'd just walked away without a word to anyone.

Daniella was living her dream, loving a man she'd never expected to find, working in this business that had been her desire since she'd been in high school and raising her daughter in the cocoon of family love. No way would Daniella willingly leave her life behind.

Marlena nearly jumped out of her chair as a loud rap sounded on the front door. Her nerves were on edge. Even though there were no guests scheduled, that didn't mean someone couldn't show up.

She relaxed as she approached the front door and saw Thomas Brady on the other side, his pleasant features radiating concern for her. She unlocked the door, and he instantly pulled her into his big arms.

"I just heard about the Connellys," he said as he continued to hold her. "I was working out of town for the past couple of days and got back home only an hour ago."

She was grateful when he finally released her and sat on the sofa in the great room. "How are you doing? Is there something I can do to help? I heard you've got a couple of FBI agents staying here. Do they have a theory on what happened?"

Marlena waited until he'd run out of breath to begin to answer his questions. "I'm doing as well as I can, although I'm terribly afraid for the family. There are three FBI agents staying here, and, no, they don't have a clue yet as to what happened and who might be responsible."

"I don't like the idea of you being here by yourself, especially with nobody knowing what happened to Sam, Daniella and Macy," Thomas said. He leaned forward, his brown eyes earnest. "You should move in with me. You would be safe under my roof."

"You know I'm not going to do that," she said softly. "Besides, I just told you there were FBI agents staying here. I also have Cory, so I'm definitely not by myself. Now tell me about the job you just finished."

Thomas was a local carpenter who not only did renovation work but also specialized in spectacular decks and patios. His skills often got him work in the larger cities in the state.

As he told her about his latest job in New Orleans, she listened absently. She had known for some time that Thomas had a thing for her. They'd even gone out on a couple of casual dates.

Sam and Daniella hadn't thought the carpenter was good enough for Marlena, but they didn't have to worry because Marlena knew her future wasn't with Thomas. She just couldn't seem to make Thomas understand that.

She enjoyed his company as a friend and thought he was a nice man, but she had no romantic feelings toward him at all. She'd told him that a hundred different ways over the past month or so, but he was still a frequent visitor and a man who obviously didn't take no easily. He seemed to think that, if she just spent enough time with him, he could change her mind about their relationship.

He couldn't. She'd rather be alone than be in a relationship without real passion, without true mutual love. Been there, done that, and the results had nearly destroyed her.

As he rambled on, Marlena realized it was the first time that he sat in the house with her. Normally Sam made it uncomfortable for the man to be anywhere but on the porch when he came to visit Marlena.

Thomas was a big man, with wide shoulders and thighs the size of tree trunks. Physical labor had given him the muscles of a bodybuilder, but he had always been gentle and soft-spoken when around her.

He had to have known that Sam and Daniella didn't approve of him. They hadn't hidden the fact that they thought he was all wrong for her.

Her heart began a slightly faster unsteady beat as she stared at the man on the sofa. Was he so obsessed with her that he had removed the people who disapproved of him? Left her alone in the house and frightened, hoping he could step in and be her support, the man she turned to in her need?

Ridiculous, a tiny voice whispered inside her. *You're looking for a bad guy in a friend who has never shown any violent tendencies, a man who has never pushed you to accept any unwanted advances.*

Still, she was grateful an hour later when he finally left with the promise to check in with her soon.

Maybe it was time she moved up her schedule for leaving Bachelor Moon.

And maybe it wasn't such a bad idea to mention Thomas's name to Gabriel.

Chapter Four

Sheriff Jim Thompson was a font of information about the history of Sam and Daniella's relationship, which had formed when Sam had come to the bed-and-breakfast for a vacation.

During that two-week stay, it had become apparent that Daniella was in danger—the first indication the murder of Samantha Walker, the daughter of Mayor Brian Walker.

It had later been determined that the bed-and-breakfast gardener, Frank Mathis, had been obsessed with Daniella and little Macy. He'd killed Samantha Walker as a gift to Daniella, because Samantha had planned on opening a bed-and-breakfast that would directly compete with Daniella's business.

Armed with this little bit of history, the three agents were now on their way to see Brian Walker. "Maybe the old man blamed Daniella for his daughter's murder and exacted some kind of revenge against the family," Jackson said as Gabriel drove down the tree-lined street that would take him to the ex-mayor's house.

"More than two years is a long time to let rage fester," Gabriel replied. "If he does have something to do with the Connellys' disappearance, then there had to have been some sort of trigger."

"A week ago was Samantha Walker's birthday," Andrew said from the backseat where he had a laptop open, checking facts.

"That could definitely be a trigger," Gabriel replied.

"There…on the left," Jackson said, pointing to the house where Brian Walker had lived for the past two years. Gabriel pulled into the driveway of the small, ill-kept house.

Weeds had long ago choked out any semblance of yard and an air of desolation hung upon the faded forest-green ranch house. Gabriel turned off the car engine and the three agents got out.

The heat was nearly overwhelming, pressing against Gabriel's chest and making it difficult to draw a deep breath. He unfastened the safety snap over his gun and knew the two agents behind him had done the same thing. They had no idea what they might be walking into. Brian Walker could be a dangerous man.

Gabriel knocked on the door, his emotions cold as he went into the survival mode that had kept him alive through many heinous cases.

It helped that he knew Jackson and Andrew had his back. He'd worked with them long enough to know they could handle almost any situation that might fly their way.

Gabriel knocked again and heard a faint cry from inside. "I'm coming. Hold your damned horses."

Gabriel drew his gun from his holster, not liking the man's tone nor his delay in opening the door.

When the door finally opened, a man in a dirty

white T-shirt and a baggy pair of black slacks stared at Gabriel and then the gun he held in his hand.

"It would be a great blessing in my life if you'd just shoot me, but I would like to know why you're doing it before you pull the trigger," he said.

Gabriel holstered his gun and instead pulled out his identification. "May we come in and have a chat with you, Mr. Walker?"

"Why not? I haven't broken any laws. Drinking too much, being slovenly and wishing yourself dead isn't a crime if it's done in the sanctity of your own home." He opened the door wider to allow them inside.

The blinds were partially pulled as if to ward off any sunshine and cheerfulness. The living room reeked of alcohol, stale cigarette smoke and old food. Gabriel's initial assessment was that Brian Walker was a man on a mission: to wish himself dead.

"Mind if my partners take a look around the house?" Gabriel asked as Brian eased into a recliner where he'd created a nest of trash around him.

"Help yourself." Brian waved airily and picked up a glass with contents that looked like scotch. "I don't suppose I could interest you in a drink."

"Thanks, but no." Gabriel lowered himself to the sofa.

"I bet I know what you're thinking," Brian said, and then took a deep swallow of his drink.

"And what's that?"

"How hard the mighty fall." Brian took another drink and then set the glass on the nearby end table. "A little over two years ago I was happily married, mayor of this little town and encouraging my beautiful, divorced daughter to follow whatever dream she had in her busy, ditzy head."

"And then Samantha was murdered," Gabriel added, his gut already telling him that this sad, broken man had nothing to do with the disappearance of the Connelly family.

Brian nodded. "And within that moment of insanity in Frank Mathis's violence, he ripped apart my entire world. A month later my wife had left me, I had resigned my position as mayor and had crawled into the bottom of a bottle and a hole that I have no desire to ever crawl out of."

"You've heard that the Connelly family is missing?" Gabriel asked.

"I heard, but if you're here because you think I had something to do with it, then you're wasting your time. I never held Daniella responsible for what happened to Samantha. Daniella was just another victim of Frank Mathis's craziness. The only difference between her and Samantha is that Daniella was lucky enough to survive his insanity."

By that time Andrew and Jackson had returned to the living room, indicating with shakes of their heads that they'd found nothing to link Brian to the Connelly family disappearance.

Minutes later the three agents were back in their car and headed out to check on another man, who Sheriff Thompson had mentioned might have reason to harm Sam Connelly.

"You can't help but feel bad for Brian Walker," Andrew said from the backseat. "Poor guy lost everything he loved—his job, his wife and his daughter."

That's why it is easier not to love, Gabriel thought. Better to keep people at bay, better to not expect kindness or love from anyone else, because when it went bad, it went so terribly bad. Certainly Gabriel had learned, at the absence of his mother's knee and at the end of his father's fist, that some people weren't meant to be loved.

"I think we can pretty much rule Brian out as a suspect," Jackson said. "I'm not sure his alcohol-addled brain could summon the cunning and savvy that our attacker had to possess in order to control the kidnapping of three people all at the same time."

"I definitely agree," Gabriel replied. "Let's see if Ryan Sherman shows a little more potential."

"Ryan Sherman, thirty-four years old," Andrew said from the backseat, once again on the laptop utilizing FBI access to the most information possible about a person.

"He spent two years in prison on an assault-and-battery charge. He's been out of the joint for the past three years and works as a mechanic at Glen's Garage," Andrew continued.

"From what Thompson told us, he and Sam have had several run-ins. Seems Ryan has a real bad attitude when it comes to the law and took a special dislike to former agent Connelly," Jackson said.

As the two of them talked about Ryan Sherman and the case, Gabriel's mind drifted to Marlena and the night before. Would she have managed to make it to shore had he not heard her scream? Somehow he doubted it. Had she been shoved off the path, or merely stumbled and imagined being pushed?

They certainly did not need another element to the mystery they'd already been handed. And the *very* last thing he needed was to think about how soft and vulnerable Marlena had looked in her robe with her damp curls framing her lovely face.

He didn't want to think about how her body had looked with her wet clothes plastered against her. In truth, he didn't want to think about her at all.

Thankfully, they arrived at Glen's Garage. As Gabriel parked on the side of the building, they were met by a man in coveralls who introduced himself as the owner, Glen Grable. "What can I do for you folks this afternoon?" he asked with an affable smile.

Gabriel flashed his identification. "We'd like to speak to Ryan Sherman."

Glen's smile transformed into a frown. "He in trouble again? Damn him. I told him, the next time I had to bail him out of jail, he was finished working here."

"We're not here to arrest him, but we do need to talk to him," Jackson said.

"Is this about the Connellys?" Glen's eyes darkened.

Gabriel took a step toward the older man. "Why would you ask? Do you know something about the Connellys?"

Glen shook his head. "Just heard that they were missing. That's all everyone in town has been talking about."

"Do you know where Ryan was on Thursday night?" Gabriel asked.

"He worked here until seven. After that I have no idea. I don't keep track of my mechanics when they're off duty. I'll go get him for you. I'd rather you talk to him out here than inside my shop where I got customers."

As they waited in the midafternoon heat, Jackson pulled a handkerchief from his back pocket and mopped his forehead. "Jeez, it's hot. It would be nice to wrap this up quickly and get back home."

Gabriel frowned. "The only way we're going to wrap this up quickly is if the family suddenly reappears alive and well, and at this point, I don't see that happening."

"I have a bad feeling about this whole thing," Andrew said softly. "I think the next time we see that family, it's going to be in a shallow grave someplace."

Andrew's words sent a somber pall over the three of them. But Gabriel knew the stats. He also knew how difficult it would be to hide three people and keep them silent and alive for any length of time.

He tensed as he watched a big, bald, tattooed man approach them. It was obvious by the sneer on his face that he wasn't happy to meet them. He was dressed in grimy coveralls and held a red grease-stained rag in his hands.

"Glen told me there were a couple of Feds out here. Just what this town needs, more Feds."

"We've heard through the grapevine that you and Sam Connelly didn't play nice together," Gabriel said.

"That sanctimonious bastard thought he was better than everyone else in town," Ryan said, and it didn't miss Gabriel's attention that he'd spoken of Sam in the past tense. "He had plans to run for sheriff after Thompson retires. I didn't want him as the new sheriff, and I let him know how I felt about it every time we ran into each other."

Ryan's brown eyes narrowed, and the snarl returned to his upper lip. "I heard he and his family are missing, and I'm sure you're here talking to me because I'm an ex-con and must be guilty of something, right? Ex-cons are always guilty of something."

"Where were you on Thursday night?" Gabriel asked, refusing to let the man's attitude get under his skin.

"I was here working."

"According to Glen, you got off work at seven."

Ryan's scowl deepened as a sheen of sweat glistened on his bald head. "I left here and went to my girlfriend's place. I spent the night there. And now if you're finished harassing me, I've got work to do."

"Your girlfriend? What's her name?" Gabriel asked.

Ryan released an irritated snort through flared nostrils. "Tammy Payne. She lives in the Bachelor Moon apartment complex. I got my own place there, too, but most nights we're together. She'll tell you I was with her all night and had nothing to do with whatever happened to the Connellys." Without waiting for a reply, Ryan stalked off back to the garage.

"What do you want to bet that Tammy tells us whatever Ryan tells her to?" Jackson asked as they headed back to their car.

"No question. But I *would* bet that Tammy Payne is either a prostitute or a stripper, because I get the feeling that's the kind of woman who'd take on a loser like Ryan. At least that's been my experience with hotheaded ex-cons, although I know there are exceptions."

Within minutes they were back in the car, the air conditioner blowing welcomed cool air as they headed to the Bachelor Moon Apartments.

"It's frustrating that Ryan Sherman is our first real person of interest in this case," Andrew said.

"Unless you count the lovely Marlena," Jackson added.

"I don't think she had anything to do with this," Gabriel said.

"Is that your professional opinion or a personal one?" Jackson asked with a raise of a dark eyebrow.

Gabriel hesitated before replying, wanting to make sure his crazy physical attraction to her had no part in his reply. "It's both," he finally said.

He hadn't mentioned Marlena's dip in the pond the night before, but he did so now, explaining to the two men how he had dragged her out of the pond.

"Do you really think somebody pushed her?" Jackson asked.

"I don't know what to believe, but she certainly believes it. What I can't figure out is if the incident is somehow tied to the disappearance of the Connellys or not. I have to ask myself if somebody wants the people associated with the bed-and-breakfast out of the way," Gabriel said.

"Out of the way of what?" Andrew asked.

Gabriel flashed him a tight smile in the rearview mirror. "I have questions, but nobody said I have any answers."

"Who is the beneficiary of the place if anything happens to Sam and Daniella?" Jackson asked.

"We need to check that out. I would assume that

initially it would have gone to Macy, with an executor or representative in place until she reaches of age. But with her missing as well, I'm not sure what would happen. I don't even know if they have a will in place." Gabriel made a mental note to check for that particular information.

By that time they had arrived at the Bachelor Moon Apartments, and they all exited the car to check out Ryan Sherman's alibi with his girlfriend.

Tammy Payne looked like she'd been ridden hard and put away wet. Lanky blond hair fell into her face as she opened the door to allow them inside. She gestured them toward the threadbare sofa and then curled her painfully thin frame into a chair facing them, but that didn't mean she sat still.

"Ryan called a little while ago to tell me to expect you," she said, first pulling on the ends of her hair and then picking at a scab on her chin. She dropped her hand to her lap but continued to fidget in junkie fashion.

"I can tell you that Ryan was here with me all night on Thursday. In fact, he's here most nights, although he has an apartment of his own."

"Is it possible he was here for a while and then maybe left while you were sleeping?" Jackson asked.

She flashed a quick smile, displaying a missing front tooth. "I don't do a lot of sleeping. So, no, that wouldn't be possible. I'll be perfectly honest. I've got a little problem with meth and Ryan is trying to help me stay on the straight and narrow." She giggled like a young girl, although she had to be in her mid-thirties. "He tells me I'm a full-time job for him."

"Have you thought about rehab?" Andrew asked.

"Been three times, and it didn't take. Ryan is the best rehab I've ever had."

The men questioned her for several minutes longer but got no more information out of her that would absolutely confirm Ryan's alibi.

"I don't think Ryan is fixing her problem, either," Jackson muttered as they left Tammy's apartment.

"No, she was definitely tweaking, but aside from that, she's crazy and dependent enough on him to provide him with an alibi for any day or time he'd need one," Gabriel said as he tightened his hands on the steering wheel.

It was dinnertime, and he headed back toward the bed-and-breakfast feeling as if their entire day had been wasted.

"I say we put Ryan Sherman on a persons of interest list," Jackson said.

"And tomorrow you can check around town and see if anyone can specify the last interaction Ryan might have had with Sam." Gabriel turned down the lane that led to the bed-and-breakfast.

"I'm just hoping Marlena has something great for dinner. I'm starving," Andrew exclaimed.

Both Jackson and Gabriel laughed. "What else is new?" Jackson replied.

As Gabriel walked up the stairs to the porch, a fist of tension knotted in his stomach as he thought of seeing Marlena.

"Hmm, something smells good," Andrew said as they entered the house.

Marlena appeared in the doorway to the dining room

and Gabriel was shocked by how the mere sight of her shot pleasure through him.

"Pot roast," she said. "And it's ready whenever you men want to eat."

"Now," Andrew said. "We're definitely ready now. They forced me to eat a sandwich from a convenience store for lunch."

Marlena laughed. "Oh, my gosh, that's a fate worse than death."

The sound of her laughter stirred a well of warmth inside Gabriel's stomach. She was a vision in pink, clad in a sundress that exposed slightly freckled slender shoulders and long bare legs.

"Give us fifteen minutes," he said and instantly turned to go upstairs. He'd scarcely gotten in the door and already felt as if he needed to distance himself from her.

Something must have been in that pond water he'd swallowed last night when he'd pulled her from its depths, for he'd had trouble keeping her out of his head all day long.

He dropped his laptop on the bed, went directly into the bathroom and sluiced cool water on his face. He had to remember that he didn't know Marlena, except that she had a slamming-hot body and the face of an angel.

But he had to stay focused on the fact that she might have something to do with what had happened to the family. He didn't know if she'd somehow manufactured a fall into the pond to complicate what was already a difficult case with few leads.

Finally, he wasn't sure that he believed that anyone could have slept through whatever had happened on the night the Connelly family disappeared. That over-turned chair indicated that they hadn't left the kitchen in utter silence.

Minutes later he joined his partners at the dining room table, where Marlena served them pot roast and vegetables, hot rolls and a salad. He was grateful that she didn't sit with them, but instead she disappeared back into the kitchen.

After dinner, Gabriel returned to his room and powered up his laptop, intending to do some background checks on all the players they'd encountered so far.

He felt as if they were no closer to having any answers than they'd been when they'd first arrived two days ago. He hated having to check in with his director and letting him know they were still clueless as to what had happened to the three people who had seemingly led a happy life here.

He gathered information and took notes, and as always, lost track of place and time as he worked. He was a man who'd always been most comfortable at work, hunting criminals and delving into the darkness of sick minds.

Maybe it was because his childhood had been a dark and frightening place, so hunting killers and cuddling up to violence felt familiar to him.

He finally closed his computer and stretched his arms overhead to work out the kinks in his shoulders. He was shocked to look at the clock and realize it was almost one in the morning.

What time had Sam, Daniella and Macy decided to have milk and cookies in the kitchen on Thursday night? He knew it had been after eight in the evening, but surely it would have been earlier than this considering Macy was only seven.

And Marlena had heard nothing.

He should go to bed. It was late, and his mind was going into strange territory. He eyed the bed, knowing that morning was going to come far too early for him.

Still, instead of heading for bed, he quietly opened his bedroom door. From the room next door he could hear the chorus of snores coming from Jackson and Andrew's room.

He crept down the stairs, the house silent around him. *It's a crazy idea,* he thought. Yet there was really only one way to prove just how soundly Marlena slept, and even though he felt a little foolish, he realized this was something he had to do for himself. He had to know.

The kitchen was lit with a small night-light plugged into an outlet next to the stove, giving him enough illumination to see that Marlena's door was closed, as he assumed it had been on the night the Connelly family had disappeared.

What he was about to do could in no way be considered an official experiment where results could be used in any way, except for as an answer to a question in his own mind. It was strictly curiosity that drove him.

He pulled out a chair from the table and pushed it so that it toppled to the floor. Then he went to the back door, unlocked it and opened it and then slammed it shut and locked it. Either noise should have awakened the woman sleeping in the next rooms, but minutes passed and she didn't fly out of her bedroom to see what was happening.

Maybe she was awake and afraid to come out of her rooms, he thought. He walked over to her door and tried the knob, surprised when it turned easily beneath his hand.

He opened the door to the darkness of her sitting room, although he saw the faint glow of another night-light coming from her bedroom.

Was she playing possum? Had she heard the noise in the kitchen and recognized what he was doing? Had she heard the sound of Sam's family being kidnapped and been too afraid to rush to help?

With quiet stealth he moved through her sitting room and stood in her bedroom doorway. She was on her side, curled up beneath the sheet. The sound of her deep, even breathing let him know she was truly asleep, that the noise he had created in the kitchen hadn't awakened her.

He should turn and leave, but instead found himself inching forward, closer to the bed. His fingers itched with the desire just to stroke softly down the side of her face, to tangle in her soft-looking curls.

As he reached the side of her bed, he wondered whether, if he pressed his lips to hers, she would awaken, like a princess responding to the kiss of her prince.

He stumbled, the ridiculous thought startling him. He backed out of her bedroom and from her apartment area. Closing the door softly behind him, he uprighted the chair he'd cast to the floor and hurried up the stairs to his bedroom.

Shutting his door, he slumped down on the bed and shook his head to dispel all thoughts of Marlena. But the action didn't work. She'd been wearing a pastel-pink nightgown, and the fragrant scent of her had filled the air. Her features had been soft and dreamy in sleep.

Why was he thinking of her as a princess and he the prince who would kiss her? He sure as hell wasn't a prince. He knew what he was—a cold man who expected no kindness, a dysfunctional man who had no desire to attempt to love anyone.

He was an FBI agent on a job and Marlena was nothing to him but a bit of fluffy distraction. If she wasn't part of this case, he'd take her to bed, satisfy the lust that ate at him and then be rid of her.

He had a family to find, a mystery to solve, and no matter the depth of his physical attraction to Marlena, he had no intention of following through on it. He just had to keep his distance from her. If he needed more information from her about the family or anything else, he'd let Jackson take over the interviewing process.

Gabriel couldn't afford to delude himself into thinking he was anyone's hero, anyone's prince. He knew the truth about himself: he had no heart and very little soul, and he'd do well to remember that.

Chapter Five

Marlena sat on the front porch, nursing a glass of iced tea and watching John and Cory work in the distance in the yard. She had spent part of the day making beds and dusting. Pamela would be in the next day to change the bedding and dust and vacuum the entire house.

Marlena hadn't made dinner tonight. She'd gotten a call from Gabriel earlier telling her the men wouldn't be home until late this evening and would eat out.

She hoped to talk to him about Thomas Brady when Gabriel returned, even though there was no possible way she could believe the affable carpenter could have anything to do with whatever had happened to the Connellys.

She'd wanted to talk to Gabriel yesterday, but he'd made himself scarce after dinner and had stayed in his room for the remainder of the night.

She took a sip of her tea and thought about the woman who would be here in the morning to clean. Pamela was usually cool and unfriendly, speaking to Marlena only when necessary and barely hiding her resentment. Marlena had learned to basically ignore the dark-haired woman and her nasty attitude.

She knew that Pamela and Daniella had been close,

especially before Marlena had arrived back in town. She also knew that Pamela saw her as an interloper who had stepped into the position of manager that Pamela had assumed would eventually be hers.

Marlena had tried to be amiable with Pamela in the first couple months after Marlena had arrived here, but when her friendly overtures had been met with disdain, she'd given up.

She now waved to Cory as he looked toward the porch, and he waved back. Her heart swelled with love for her brother. Oh, there were days she wanted to knock him in the head, but he was basically a good kid at heart.

Where was little Macy with her diva attitude and silly antics? Where were Sam and Daniella? Marlena's heart ached with their absence with an all-encompassing fear for them.

Sunset had just begun to splash gorgeous colors across the sky when Gabriel pulled up and parked. She could tell by the body language of all three men that it had been a frustrating day for them.

Jackson and Andrew nodded to her and went inside, but as Gabriel followed she halted him by calling his name. "Could I talk to you for a minute?" she asked and gestured to the wicker chair close to hers.

He frowned as if he found her request unpleasant, but sank into the chair with a weary sigh. "What's going on?" he asked.

"I thought of somebody else you might want to check out," she said.

He sat up straighter in the chair, the tired lines on his face seeming to magically disappear. "Who?"

Marlena hesitated a moment, wondering if she was creating problems for a man who'd done absolutely nothing wrong. "His name is Thomas Brady."

"And what exactly does he have to do with the bed-and-breakfast or Sam and Daniella?"

"Actually not much. It's more that he has something to do with me."

Gabriel's eyes darkened. "What do you mean?"

"Why don't I get you some lemonade, and then I'll explain." As he nodded his assent, she jumped out of her chair and hurried inside. She poured him a tall glass of the cold liquid and told herself that she was doing the right thing by mentioning Thomas. The last thing she wanted was to be responsible for not giving them information that might prove valuable.

When she returned to the porch, she handed him the drink and then returned to her chair, aware of him watching her intently as the purple shadows of twilight began to fall.

"Thomas Brady is a local carpenter who has made it clear that he wants to have a romantic relationship with me. We went out a couple of times, but for me the relationship has never been anything but a friendship. But Thomas has been persistent, and he believes we belong together."

In the deepening shadows Gabriel's features looked sharper, a little bit dangerous. "So what could your relationship with Thomas have to do with the Connellys' disappearance?"

Marlena paused to take a sip of her lemonade. She set the glass on the wicker table between them and released a sigh. "Sam and Daniella don't like Thomas, and they've made their feelings toward him fairly clear. They don't think he's good enough for me. They don't want to see us together as a couple. They've always been cool to Thomas when he's come here to visit with me."

She frowned and looked out to where John and Cory were loading up their gardening tools into a wheelbarrow. "Thomas stopped by yesterday, and we visited for a little while. He was more at ease than he'd ever been, with Sam and Daniella not around." She shrugged. "He suggested it would be safer for me if I moved in with him. I just thought you should maybe check him out. He was supposedly out of town working on a deck in New Orleans when the family disappeared."

"I will check him out," Gabriel replied. He took a drink of his lemonade and leaned back in the chair, looking nothing if not exhausted.

"Bad day?" she asked sympathetically.

"Bad case," he replied. He looked out to where John and Cory headed to the gardening shed. They stopped suddenly, and John grabbed a hoe and began to smack the ground.

"What's he doing?" Gabriel asked.

"Must have stumbled across another snake. We have a nest of rattlesnakes and way too many cottonmouths on the grounds, and John is our official snake killer. Cory would rather try to catch them. He loves snakes and reptiles, but John has a healthy fear of them and always cuts off their heads."

They both watched as John picked up on the hoe what was obviously now a dead snake and tossed it into the wheelbarrow.

"I hate snakes," Gabriel admitted. "I'd rather face a perp with a gun than stumble on a snake."

She released a small laugh. "I'd rather not face either of those situations."

"Your brother seems like a good kid."

"He's a pretty normal kid. And by that I mean one day I want to kiss him to death and the next day I want to wring his neck," she admitted and was rewarded with a brief smile from Gabriel. "What about you? What kind of a kid were you when you were around Cory's age?"

"Tough. I was basically living on the streets, working at a fast-food joint to get by."

"Where were your parents?" she asked.

His features took on a dark and dangerous mask. "My mother took off for parts unknown when I was seven, leaving me in the custody of the meanest bastard in the state of Mississippi—my father. I lived in constant fear of him from the time my mother left until I left home at sixteen."

He paused and took another sip of his lemonade. "That's why I had my window open the other night, because from the time I was a little kid, I had to have an escape route from my old man." He was silent for a moment and then jerked, as if pulling his thoughts back to the present.

"After I left home, for the next couple of years I did whatever I needed to do to survive on my own."

"So how did you wind up as an FBI agent?" What she wanted to say was that she was sorry for what he'd gone through with his father, that her heart ached for the little boy he had been, but she knew he'd hate her for going there.

"A street cop got friendly with me and encouraged me to finish school, get into college, and that's when the FBI tapped me on the shoulder. And here I am, working on the right side of the law."

"Funny, we have similar backgrounds. I think I mentioned before that my mother took off when Cory was young. The truth of the matter is she discovered she loved drugs more than she loved her husband and her kids. Cory was about four when my father told her she had to leave. She came around a couple more times after that looking for money, and when my father refused to give her any, she finally disappeared for good."

She picked up her glass and finished the last of her lemonade. "One of the final times she came to the house, I remember she hugged me and told me how much she loved me and then asked me for my allowance. I was so mad at her that I told her I never wanted to see her again, and I didn't. My dad tried to hold it together, but when Cory was thirteen, he died of a heart attack."

Her whole body ached as she remembered those moments when her mother had held her close, stroking her hair and telling her how much she loved her. She had so wanted to believe, had needed to believe that her mother had changed and their family would be put back together. When her mother had asked for Marlena's allowance money, it had irrevocably broken any mother-daughter bond that might have survived.

"I guess we both got tough breaks," he said. His features were no longer visible in the darkness that had finally claimed the area.

For a few minutes they sat in silence, and Marlena wondered what he was thinking. What scars had been left behind by his mother's absence and father's brutality? By life itself?

"You think they're dead, don't you?" she asked. It had been a question that had tormented her since the morning she'd awakened to find Sam, Daniella and Macy gone; a question she'd been afraid to ask until this very moment.

"It's possible that they're still alive. We can always hope for the best," he answered after a long hesitation.

She was grateful that it was dark enough that she couldn't see his features, for she heard the lie in his voice but was glad she didn't have to see it in his eyes.

Minutes later, after he'd gone inside, Marlena remained in the chair, watching the fireflies begin to take over the area. Tears blurred her vision as she remembered Macy chasing the flashing bugs and her squeals of delight when she managed to capture one in a jar.

How Marlena wished Macy was out there now, chasing fireflies, her laughter filling the air. How she wished Daniella and Sam were sitting on the porch with her, enjoying the last of the evening before bedtime.

As the sound of bullfrogs rose in the air, a shiver swept up her spine as she thought of her plunge into the pond. She no longer knew if she'd really been pushed or had stumbled and fallen off the path and into the lake. It all felt like a bad dream now, unclear and fuzzy.

But the night air suddenly felt fraught with danger, and she quickly jumped up from her chair and went inside, even knowing that for Sam and Daniella and little Macy, the house hadn't been a safe haven.

SUNDAY EVENING GABRIEL told his two agents to take the next day off. Their Sunday had been a long one, and he felt as if they all needed a little downtime to clear their heads.

On Monday morning, Gabriel was still in bed when Jackson and Andrew knocked on his door and asked if he wanted to go with them for breakfast at a café in town. He declined, but as he went downstairs to the dining room and heard Marlena humming from the kitchen, he was sorry he hadn't gone with his two partners.

As he poured himself a cup of coffee from the pot in the dining room, he realized he liked the sound of her humming. It was an unfamiliar but pleasant feminine noise he'd never enjoyed before.

He followed it into the kitchen and paused and watched as she stirred a big pot of what smelled like rich spaghetti sauce. He noticed that her bottom wiggled with each stir of the big spoon.

"I checked out your boyfriend last night," he said.

She whirled around, obviously startled by his presence. "You scared me." She placed the spoon in the spoon rest. "And he's not my boyfriend." She grabbed a cup of coffee that was on the nearby counter, then sat at the table and motioned for him to join her.

He hesitated. He could smell her scent, clean from a morning shower, sprayed with the fresh floral fragrance that had imprinted itself into his head. Her scent, combined with the tomato-and-herb odor of the sauce, somehow brought to his mind what home might smell like.

Stop it, he mentally commanded himself. He sat at the table and tried to staunch the alien thoughts that drifted through his mind.

She sat across from him and looked at him expectantly. "So what did you find out about Thomas, and how on earth did you do it so quickly?"

"Ah, the wonder of the internet and the magic of the FBI's powers." He paused to take a drink of his coffee and then continued. "Thomas Brady, thirty-seven years old. Never married, no criminal background—the man appears on paper to be squeaky clean."

"That's good to know."

"I still need to have a face-to-face meeting with him and check out his alibi. Just because somebody has managed to keep a clean record doesn't necessarily mean he's not a bad guy."

Marlena frowned, the dainty line dancing in the center of her forehead doing nothing to detract from her beauty. "I can't imagine Thomas being so upset that he would do something terrible to the family." She got up from her chair. "You want some breakfast? I've got bacon already cooked, and it would take me just a minute to fry up a couple of eggs."

"Okay, if it isn't too much trouble," he replied. Maybe he would find her less distracting if she was doing something instead of sitting across from him and gazing at him with her amazing eyes.

"Sam and Daniella never talked about having a will?" he asked as she moved across the room to the refrigerator.

"Never. It wasn't something we would have talked about." She carried the egg carton to the counter next to the stove. "Scrambled, over easy or hard cooked?" she asked.

"Scrambled is fine. Pamela seemed to think that if Sam and Daniella had a will, then Macy would be a beneficiary and so would you."

Marlena laughed and turned to face him. "I told you before, there's no way I would be in any will. Daniella would never do that. This bed-and-breakfast was her dream from the time she was a teenager, but she knew it was never mine." She turned back around to the counter and placed two slices of bread in the toaster, then moved an iron skillet over a heating burner.

"Daniella knew that my plan in the next couple of months was to move to either Baton Rouge or New Orleans. She and Sam paid me a good wage, and I've managed to squirrel away most of it so I can go to college and get my teaching degree. I've even made Cory put half of his paycheck each week into a savings account so that when we get to the city, he can enroll in a trade school. Daniella would have never left me this place because she knew I wouldn't want it."

She looked at him again with a wry smile. "I guess that removes me as a suspect with a financial motive."

"You've pretty much been taken off my suspect list anyway," he replied.

"Thanks. I appreciate your clarity."

He was surprised by the small burst of laughter that escaped him. "That's about the only clarity I've had about this case so far."

She turned back around, and as she tended to his

breakfast, they fell into silence. He sipped his coffee and stared out the window where a flower bed exploded with a variety of colorful blooms.

"John came up clean, too," he said as she set his plate before him and then rejoined him at the table. "What do you know about him?"

She shrugged, her bare, faintly freckled shoulders enchanting him. "I know he's from New Orleans but used to work for some big hotel in Shreveport, and was looking for a change of pace and a smaller town. When he saw the ad that Sam had run in the paper, he applied for the job and then came here for a visit."

"Apparently Sam liked what he saw in the young man," Gabriel said as he picked up a slice of his toast.

"I like what I see in John. He's been like a big brother to Cory, and he seems to know everything there is to know about plants and trees and flowers. I think he has a degree in horticulture. He came here with a glowing recommendation from his former job." She frowned. "Surely he isn't on your suspect list. Sam and John got along great, and he was considered part of the family."

Gabriel fell silent as he ate his breakfast, his thoughts going over what little they knew about the disappearance. He had no idea specifically what time the family had vanished. They had now been missing over three days, and his hope to find them alive was shrinking.

"Our suspect list stinks, we have no real leads to follow and we're no closer to figuring out what happened to the family than we were when we first arrived," he said with disgust. He shoved his empty plate aside and reached for his coffee cup.

Marlena got up and went for his plate, but before she grabbed it, she laid her hand over the back of his. His heart stopped as she gazed at him, her smaller hand warm over his.

He fought an impulse to snatch his hand away, unaccustomed to anyone touching him for any reason. She offered him a smile of encouragement. "You're going to figure this out, Gabriel. I just know you and your men are going to get to the bottom of things." She gave his hand a quick squeeze and then released it, leaving him feeling oddly bereft.

As she moved to the sink with his plate, he once again stared out the window, his thoughts jumbled with both the crime and her. She topped up their coffee and then sat across from him.

"Tell me about the people on your suspect list," she said.

"To be honest, we don't even have a real suspect list at the moment. All we have is a person of interest list."

"Then tell me about your persons of interest."

He leaned back in the chair. "Your boyfriend, until I can check his alibi." He'd deliberately called Thomas that to get her reaction.

His reward was the flash of aggravation in her delicious green eyes. "He is not my boyfriend." She must have seen a spark of something in his eyes, for she suddenly grinned. "Ah, the big dark FBI agent does have a sense of humor after all."

"I have my moments," he said easily. "In any case,

for now Thomas Brady is on my list, along with Ryan Sherman."

"I'd forgotten about Ryan," she said. "He's a thug, a creep, and he hated Sam with a passion. Of course, he hates anyone who has anything to do with law enforcement."

"The problem is that Ryan has an alibi. He was supposedly with his girlfriend the night of the disappearance. The other issue is, if somebody took the family and is keeping them alive, then they have to have a place for them. There's no way Ryan would be keeping hostages in his dinky apartment. Jackson spent some time Saturday morning at City Hall checking to see if Ryan owns any other property in the area, but we came up with nada."

"His parents own some property out in the boondocks. I think Ryan does mechanic work on the side in an old shed out there."

"You have an address?" Gabriel asked.

"No, but I can give you directions."

He held up his finger and then pulled his cell phone from his pocket. He called Jackson and explained the situation to him, and then put Marlena on the phone to give him the directions.

"Check it out and get back to me," he said to Jackson when Marlena handed his phone back to him.

"We're on it," Jackson replied, and then the two men disconnected. Gabriel pocketed his cell phone, but was surprised to realize he wasn't in a hurry to leave the kitchen or Marlena.

He told himself it was because she might hold some nugget of information that could advance the case, such as the fact that Ryan's parents owned a place where perhaps people could be stashed. Who knew what other little tidbits she had that she didn't even realize might be helpful for finding anyone who posed a threat to the family.

He told himself he was here at the table with her because he still believed she was part of the key to solving the mystery of whatever happened to the Connellys.

He assured himself it had nothing to do with the sunshine in her curls, the graceful motion she displayed when she got out of her chair to stir the sauce and then return to the table or the warmth of her smile when she gazed at him.

"We know they weren't taken for ransom because we haven't received any kind of a money demand for their safe return," he said, trying to focus on business and not the pleasure of her company.

"Who would pay any kind of ransom? Neither Sam nor Daniella had family, and although this place holds its own, they aren't exactly millionaires," she replied.

"I keep thinking there had to be more than one perp. Otherwise how could a single person control three people at the same time, one of them a seasoned FBI agent?"

"Simple," she replied. "It was love that kept them easily controlled."

He looked at her curiously, wondering if she was being silly, but her eyes held a glow of knowing, of certainty that told him she was being serious.

"Love?" Disbelief laced his tone.

"All it would take would be a single person getting through the back door and putting a gun to Sam's head. Daniella and Macy would instantly become compliant to whatever he told them to do. It would be the same thing if somebody threatened Daniella or Macy. It would only take a threat to any one of them to effectively neutralize the others because of their enormous love for one another."

"I've never experienced that kind of love for or from anyone," he said.

She gazed at him for several long moments, her eyes holding a wealth of emotion. "That's the saddest thing I've ever heard."

He felt the need to escape, run from the faint pity in her eyes, the cozy atmosphere of the kitchen and the feeling that somehow he was missing an integral piece of what made up a human being.... He was missing a heart.

Chapter Six

For the next several days Marlena scarcely saw the three agents who were living in the house. They ate a quick breakfast each morning and then took off for town to sniff out whatever they could about the disappearance.

There had been nothing on Ryan Sherman's parents' acreage to indicate that the Connellys had ever been there. Even though they had considered Brian Walker, the ex-mayor, as a nonplayer, they'd checked his finances to make sure he hadn't made a big withdrawal that would indicate the possibility of a kidnapping or killing for hire.

Marlena learned bits and pieces about the investigation as she served them their meals each evening. Since that long-ago morning in the kitchen, Gabriel hadn't sought her out for any conversations, and instead he had distanced himself from her.

She told herself it didn't matter, that he meant nothing to her. Besides, they were obviously two people with very different ideas about love.

Marlena wanted—needed—to believe that eventually she would be deeply in love with somebody who loved her back. She wanted the husband and the house, a couple of kids and a dog. Love had already kicked her hard in the butt while she'd been living in Chicago, but that hadn't turned her off the idea of everlasting love; it had only made her yearn for it more.

But love hadn't saved Sam and Daniella and Macy. Somebody had possibly manipulated their love for each other to do harm. And with each day that passed, she couldn't imagine who that person might be.

Thomas's alibi still hung in the balance as far as Gabriel, Andrew and Jackson were concerned. Although records showed that Thomas had checked into a motel in New Orleans for a week prior to the disappearance, and he had worked on a deck for a family residence, there were increments of time missing when Thomas couldn't tell the FBI exactly where he'd been or what he'd been doing.

Considering the approximate time of night that the disappearance had occurred, it was possible he would have had enough leeway to drive back to Bachelor Moon, do something with the family and then be at his motel again for the breakfast buffet the next morning.

She could feel the frustration of the agents each night when they settled in the dining room for the evening meal, a frustration that let her know they were no closer to solving the mystery.

How long could they remain here trying to solve a crime that had no clues? With no trails to follow? When would this become a cold case with no answers, and when did somebody decide for sure that it had changed from an open investigation to a hunt for bodies?

It had been a week ago tonight that the Connellys had disappeared, leaving behind empty glasses of milk and uneaten cookies. Marlena knew from the FBI inquiries that their bank accounts hadn't been touched, their ATMs and credit cards hadn't been accessed. The family was just…gone.

And how long did she and Cory stay here? Wondering, hoping that Sam and Daniella and Macy would magically walk through the front door and declare that it had all been a joke, a spur-of-the-moment vacation?

As she fixed the evening meal of roasted chicken and vegetables, she listened for the front door, knowing that if the agents stayed true to their schedule of the past few days, they should be walking in any minute.

It was crazy how much she'd missed the quiet moments of conversation with Gabriel. He not only drew her on a physical level, but since she'd seen a glimpse into his past, he drew her on an emotional level, too. But she knew that was dangerous to her own mental health.

He was a man who didn't believe in love, and she was a woman who desperately believed and wanted that in her life. He obviously had no desire for home and hearth, and the desire for such a thing was integral to who she was as a woman.

She'd just pulled the chicken and veggies out of the oven when she heard the front door open. Setting the large pan of food on a cooling rack, she left the kitchen and went through the great room to see all three men wearing the wearied expressions of another fruitless day.

"Dinner is ready whenever you all want to eat," she said. Although she spoke to all three, her gaze lingered on Gabriel. His eyes held the darkness of frustration, and the lines of his face indicated not just a physical weariness but a soul-deep weariness, as well.

What she wanted to do was walk to him and pull him into her arms. What she wanted to do was caress the tired lines that creased across his forehead, to do something that would ease some of the torment he obviously felt.

"Give us fifteen minutes to wash up, and then we'll be down," Andrew said, already heading up the stairs.

As the other men followed him, Marlena turned and went back into the kitchen. The table in the dining room was already set, so she placed the two chickens on a big serving plate and the veggies in a large dish, and carried them to the table with her first two trips. She'd also made a cherry Jell-O salad and hot, yeasty rolls.

With the entire meal on the table, she returned to the kitchen and poured herself a glass of iced tea, then sat at the kitchen table and stared out the window.

They were all in a state of limbo, waiting for people who might never return, afraid to leave without answers. She'd planned to head to one of the bigger cities with Cory in the next couple of months, but wondered if maybe she needed to move up their plans to go.

Pamela would be thrilled to take over the daily running of the bed-and-breakfast in Daniella's absence, and Marlena knew the woman was competent enough to make sure it was all done to Daniella's high standards.

No will had been found in any of the paperwork Sam kept in the office. So what would happen to this place if Daniella and Sam never returned?

Long after dinner was over and she'd cleaned up the kitchen, she carried a glass of iced tea out to one of the wicker rockers on the porch. Cory had stopped in earlier to let her know that he and John were going to the movies to see the latest action-adventure release that was playing.

As always, Marlena thanked the stars for John's friendship with her brother. Cory would have gone stark raving mad here if not for John's company.

She rocked the wicker chair and sipped her tea as she watched the sun dip lower in the sky. "No place are the sunsets prettier than in Louisiana," Gabriel said as he stepped out on the porch, a glass of tea in his hand.

She sat up straighter, surprised by his appearance as he eased into the chair next to hers. Instantly she was overwhelmed by the scent of minty soap, shaving cream and that now-familiar woodsy cologne, letting her know he'd recently taken a shower.

"I think the sunsets here in Bachelor Moon are pretty spectacular, because they don't have to fight with city skylines or bright lights," she replied.

"Dinner was delicious."

She smiled at him. "Thanks. I don't claim to be a professional chef, but thank goodness Daniella has some great cookbooks and all I have to do is follow directions."

He placed his tea on the table between them and then rubbed the center of his forehead, as if to ease his pain. "Headache?" she asked sympathetically.

He nodded and dropped his hand to his lap. "I woke up with it this morning, and it's been relentless."

"Want some aspirin or something?"

"No, thanks. I know it's just a bad case of stress." He released a deep sigh. "This has been the case from hell. We've spent the past week spinning our wheels and getting little information for our efforts. I even checked to make sure Frank Mathis is still in prison."

"He is, isn't he?"

"He's safe behind bars and completely out of the picture for whatever happened here a week ago."

"It feels like they've been gone forever," Marlena said, her throat closing up as she felt the imminence of tears. "I can't imagine them not being in my life in one way or another."

"I wish I could promise you a happy ending," he said softly. "But to be perfectly honest, I don't have a clue how this all might end. I think this may be one of the most frustrating cases I've ever worked."

"I just wish I could be of more help, but I've gone over and over it in my mind, and I can't think of anyone who would have the capacity or the desire to kidnap Sam, Daniella and Macy." Her voice cracked slightly with emotion and she reached for her tea as if a swallow would wash away the pain in her heart.

She took a drink and then cleared her throat. "What happens if you don't find out the answers? How long will your director allow you to work a case where there are no clues, no leads to follow?"

"I don't know. Right now he's given us no indication he wants us pulled off the case." He sat up a little taller in the chair. "The one thing I've learned while doing this work is that you never know when a clue will drop in your lap, when something will occur or some information will be learned that forms a lead.

We've only had a week, and in the world of criminal investigations that's just a minute."

As the sun began to fully dip below the horizon and the shadows of night crept in, Marlena stood, taking her tea glass with her. "Since the night of my impromptu swim, I'm no longer comfortable sitting out here when it gets dark."

"Do you still think somebody intentionally shoved you in the pond?" He grabbed his glass and also rose from his chair.

She frowned thoughtfully. "I'm not sure right now what I think about that night. It's possible that I was so freaked out by the family's disappearance that I imagined I was pushed when I actually just stepped the wrong way."

"You haven't felt threatened by anyone or anything since then?" he asked.

She realized they stood too close to each other, that his eyes, normally midnight blue and so hard to read, appeared softer in the glow of twilight.

"No, nothing." She turned quickly and went into the house. He followed behind her, and as she placed her glass in the kitchen sink, he did the same.

They were close together, facing each other in what felt like a void of time, of space. She knew she should say good-night and move away, but she was frozen in place, unable to speak, unable to move. His close proximity to her made her feel trapped, forbidden to escape even if she'd wanted to.

Her heart thundered as he took a step closer to her. "I've been fighting the need to do this since I first saw you on the front porch a week ago." His voice was a mere whisper as he raised a hand and drew it softly through her curls.

He nodded as if satisfied. "I knew it would be soft as silk." He dropped his hand from her hair and instead ran his thumb across her bottom lip. "I've also wanted to do this since the moment I saw you."

Before she could draw a breath or prepare in any way for what she knew was about to happen, his mouth covered hers in a fiery kiss that was directly at odds with the dispassionate man she'd thought him to be.

He tasted of sweetened tea and hot desire, and she opened her mouth to him as his arms wrapped around her and pulled her close.

A little voice inside her head told her this shouldn't be happening, but it was happening, and it was wonderful. His body was solid against hers, and she instantly knew he was aroused.

Their tongues battled together as if desperate to explore and know each other, as if both of them knew this explosion of simmering lust that had existed between them would never happen again, culminating in this, their first and last kiss.

It was he who broke the kiss, dropping his arms from around her and jumping back as if she were on fire.

His ragged breathing matched her own as he stared at her. "I just had to know," he said. "And now I do, and that won't happen again." Without waiting for her response, he turned and left the kitchen.

GABRIEL SAT IN the Rusty Nail Tavern just off Main Street in Bachelor Moon, nursing a beer alone at the end of the counter. Most of the people who shared the space with him knew that he was one of the FBI agents who'd come to town to investigate the Connellys' disappearance, and he knew that most of them didn't like the fact that he'd invaded their space.

He wasn't a native. He wasn't one of them. Nobody approached him, and that was just fine with him. He was doing what he did best—watching people, eavesdropping on conversations, perfectly satisfied being alone.

It had been two nights since he'd kissed Marlena and he was still trying to get the taste of her out of his mouth. He took a drink of his beer as if that would do the trick, and his gaze constantly moved over the Saturday-night crowd.

Was the perp in the room right now? Silently crowing over how easily he'd managed to fool the agents who had been sent here to investigate? Gabriel tightened his hand around the neck of his beer bottle. Within days it would be two full weeks since the Connelly family had last been seen, and they were no closer to having any answers.

This case was driving him crazy. *She* was driving him crazy. That kiss had been one of the biggest mistakes he'd ever made in his life, for now it was emblazoned on his brain, and he couldn't stop thinking about kissing her again.

He took another pull of his beer, wondering if they were ever going to get a break on this case. For the past couple of days, he and Andrew and Jackson had beat feet across the town, checking abandoned storefronts, empty storage units, old barns and sheds, anywhere that a family of three could be stashed away and any-place bodies could have been disposed.

They'd listened to gossip, to rumors and had chased down a dozen dead ends. With each day that passed, his belief that the Connelly family was alive had slowly died. He believed it was just a matter of time before their bodies were discovered by somebody walking in a field, strolling through a forest or fishing near a swamp.

What he found hard to accept was that it was possible he and his small team of two would leave here and never have any answers, never know who was responsible.

If he looked deep inside himself, he also knew that he found it hard to believe he would leave here without following through on that steamy kiss he'd stolen from Marlena.

He wanted more.

He wanted a lot more from her.

He wanted to slide his mouth down her neck, cup her bare breasts in his hands while she moaned in acquiescence. It had nothing to do with love or romance. It had nothing to do with anything but the raging lust she created inside him.

What made it so difficult to get out of his head was the fact that he thought she felt the same way about him. She'd eagerly accepted his kiss, had pressed herself against him as if she'd been willing to give him more. And he'd wanted to take more.

"Smells like pig in here—a big fat federal pig," a deep voice said from nearby.

Gabriel turned to see Ryan Sherman and his girl-friend, Tammy, seated at a table for two near the bar. Gabriel whirled around on his bar stool and stared at them. He mentally groaned. He was in no mood to deal with a yahoo. Ryan apparently didn't realize he was baiting a pit bull.

Gabriel continued to stare at Ryan, almost begging him to do something stupid so Gabriel could fly into action and get rid of the energy building inside him. But Tammy placed a hand on Ryan's arm and whispered in his ear, and Ryan broke the intense, challenging stare, and instead got up and wandered toward the pool tables on the other side of the room.

Gabriel turned around, finished his beer and checked his watch. Nearly midnight. The crowd had begun to thin out a bit, and he knew if he had one more beer, it would be one too many to drive back to the bed-and-breakfast. It was time to leave.

He hadn't invited Andrew or Jackson to come along with him to the tavern. As much as he liked them, he'd needed a break from them, too. They would be in their room by now, their deep snores mingling to create a discordant form of music.

As he left the bar, the night air wrapped around him, thick and humid and with the tang of ozone that preceded an approaching storm. As he got into the car, he saw in the distance a zigzag of lightning split the darkness of the black, clouded sky.

If he was lucky, he would make it to the bed-and-breakfast before the storm hit. Driving with his window down, breathing in the heavy, thick air, the distant rumble of thunder pealed and he stepped on the gas, eager to get inside before the wind and rain arrived.

He felt as if the storm was inside of him, and he understood the interior tumult mirrored the unstable atmosphere around him. He also knew the genesis of his unhinged emotions.

Marlena.

It had only been nine days since he'd met her, and yet he felt as if he'd wanted her for an entire lifetime, as if he had been born wanting her, and he wouldn't be satisfied until he had her.

It's the beer talking, he tried to tell himself as he pulled up in front of the house and parked the car. He got out of the vehicle and stood, taking several deep breaths of the wildness of the night around him, flinching slightly as a slash of lightning slivered brilliantly in the stormy skies. It was followed within seconds by a loud clap of thunder, letting him know the storm was nearly upon him.

He used the key Marlena had given him to enter through the front door quietly. He relocked it behind him, but before going upstairs, he needed a big glass of water. He'd learned a long time ago that the best chaser for too many beers was water. It helped to keep a morning hangover to a minimum.

He crept through the darkness of the great room and dining room, guided by the small night-light in the kitchen.

Stepping into the kitchen, he froze at the sight of Marlena standing in front of the opened refrigerator door, clad only in a short filmy pink nightgown. As if sensing his presence, she closed the refrigerator, her eyes wide as she looked at him.

Lightning flashed in the room as he took several steps toward her, unable to stop himself even if he'd wanted to. He felt as if the wicked hand of fate was at work, and he was helpless not to follow where it led.

Without saying a word, he approached where she stood with her hand pressed against the fridge. He placed his palms on either side of her on the cool white exterior of the appliance, his arms effectively trapping her in place.

He was wild with want, and couldn't help but notice that her breasts rose and fell in a rapid rhythm that matched the quickened beating of his heart. Her nipples were outlined against the thin material of her nightgown as if to taunt him, as if inviting his touch.

"Are you drunk?" she finally asked, her voice husky and breathless.

"Apparently not drunk enough," he replied, and then took her mouth with his as he pressed against her. If she was smart, she'd smell the wildness on him, run from it... Run from him.

But she apparently wasn't smart, for instead of running away from him, she looped her arms around his neck, pulled him closer and opened her mouth to him.

He was vaguely aware of thunder and lightning and rain beginning to pelt the windows, and then he was conscious of nothing but kissing Marlena.

Her soft floral scent surrounded him, invading his senses to the point that nothing else mattered but her. He would have her tonight. He knew it by the fire in her kiss, by the way her body met his in mindless yearning.

He would have her tonight, and then this desperate wanting of her would finally be satiated, and he'd be done with her haunting his thoughts, invading his dreams.

Chapter Seven

Marlena had known she was in trouble the minute she'd seen him in the kitchen doorway. A primal energy had wafted from him, an energy that fed one inside of her.

She knew what he wanted, and she wanted it, too. From the moment he had kissed her two nights before, she'd known that eventually they would make love. *No, not make love,* she mentally corrected herself. She'd known they would have sex.

She wouldn't delude herself into believing that what they were about to do had anything to do with love. He was a man who couldn't love, but still she somehow knew he could take her to sexual splendor, and at the moment that was enough.

It was the last rational thought she had as Gabriel's lips plied hers with fire, and he ground his hips against hers, letting her know he was already fully aroused.

There had been instant tension between them from the moment they'd first met, and now she recognized that it had been physical desire, a desire nearly impossible to deny even if she had wanted to.

As his lips left hers and blazed a slow trail down her throat, she tangled her fingers through his thick dark hair and whispered his name.

He leaned back and looked at her, as if expecting her to tell him this was enough, that he needed to go to his room now and stop what they both knew was about to happen.

"Come with me to my room," she said, taking any doubt out of the situation.

He stepped back from her, his eyes glowing as another flash of lightning momentarily lit the room. "Are you sure?" His voice was taut with tension.

As a reply she took his hand firmly in hers and led him into her private quarters. He stood in the center of the sitting room as she locked the door, and then he followed her into the bedroom, where a small lamp pooled a glow from the nightstand.

She turned, and before she could say anything or draw a single breath, she was back in his arms, his mouth covering hers in a kiss that seared her to her very core.

They fell onto her bed, their embrace unbroken, his mouth still covering hers. The tumult of the storm was personified in her bedroom, barely restrained, as he fumbled with his buttons to remove his shirt.

She helped him, wanting to feel his naked chest, to run her fingers across his warm, firm muscles. When his shirt was finally undone, he broke the kiss, sat up, shrugged out of the shirt and threw it into the darkness beyond the bed.

She watched hungrily as he stepped from the bed, kicked off his shoes and pulled off his socks then removed his slacks, leaving him clad only in a pair of black boxers. The light from the bedside table loved his skin, emphasizing lean muscle and wiry strength. With eyes that glittered with unbridled need, he returned to the bed and pulled her back into his arms.

His skin was fevered as his legs wound around hers, and she grabbed hold of his broad, bare shoulders. They kissed again, his mouth feeling as if he touched her everywhere.

He broke the kiss and stared at her, the faint light dancing silver shards in the depths of his blue eyes. "You know that tomorrow it will be as if all of this never happened."

She heard the words he didn't say, words to let her know this night meant nothing to him, that it wasn't the beginning or the end of anything. It just was.

She nodded. "I know, and that's okay with me."

It was as if these simple words unleashed the most powerful part of the storm. He grabbed the hem of her nightgown and pulled it up and off her, leaving her clad only in a small pair of matching panties.

"You are so beautiful," he said, his voice deep and husky as his gaze lingered on her bare breasts. He cupped them with his hands and rubbed his thumbs over her nipples until they were taut and aching. "I haven't been able to get you out of my mind."

When he drew one of her nipples into his mouth, a moan of pleasure escaped her. He teased the tip, licking and sucking as she tangled her hands in his hair and pulled him closer, tighter against her.

In all of her twenty-seven years, she'd never known the need she felt at this moment, never experienced the kind of out-of-control passion she felt now for him... for Gabriel.

As he continued to tease and lick her nipples, first

one and then the other, one of his hands slid down the flat of her stomach. Her breath caught as he rubbed his hand over her intimately, the only barrier the silk panties she still wore.

His hand heated the silk, and she arched her hips up to encourage the contact. She was on fire, and he was the only person who could put out her flame.

She reached down and wrapped her hand around his hard length, shielded only by the cotton of his boxers. He released a groan as she squeezed slightly and moved her hand up and down.

He allowed her to continue for only moments, and then rolled away from her and took off his boxers. This time when he kissed her, he started in the center of her breasts and nipped and licked downward.

She stopped breathing in anticipation as his mouth moved along her stomach and then whispered across her panties, warming her with his breath. He removed her panties by inches as she raised her hips to aid him. When his mouth touched her there, she climaxed and cried his name again and again.

As she came back to earth, he hovered between her thighs, his boxers gone, his face taut and beautiful with his need for her.

She grabbed his tight butt and pulled him forward, reveling in his need, welcoming her own. He slid into her with a deep sigh, and then his lips found hers in a kiss of aching tenderness.

He ended the kiss and then began to stroke, slow and deep inside her. Their breaths became pants as his motions became faster, more frantic, and she felt the rise of exquisite pleasure building again inside her.

She clung to him, encouraging the piston of him rubbing against her, into her, until she flew over the edge at the same time he stiffened with his own release.

They remained locked together, their breathing ragged as faint thunder sounded, indicating that the storm had passed. He finally moved off her and stood. He grabbed his boxers from the floor and stepped into them, then grabbed his shirt and pants, as well.

"Just think of this as a dream you had," he said, and then he was gone from the bedroom. A moment later she heard the sound of the door leading to the kitchen open, then close.

She remained in bed, satiated and drowsy and feeling like it had all been some sort of crazy dream. But the scent of him lingered on her sheets, and her body still retained his imprint.

Reluctantly she got out of bed, picked up her panties and nightgown from the floor and went into the bathroom. Minutes later she was back in bed, but sleep was the last thing on her mind.

She'd awakened earlier and felt hungry. She'd been staring at the contents of the refrigerator trying to decide on a late-night snack when he'd appeared, and any appetite she might have had for food had disappeared.

Her head was filled with Gabriel. Although she had told him she'd pretend they'd never had sex, that this night would mean nothing in the light of dawn, she knew she had lied.

Although she had no expectations from him, understood that this night would remain just a single night of hot sex in his mind, she would hold it tight in her heart to be remembered whenever she thought about how fragile life could be, how haunted she'd felt when Sam and Daniella and little Macy had disappeared.

She would retain this memory inside her mind, inside her heart, because being in Gabriel's arms tonight had made her feel safe and loved, even though she knew it had been a false illusion.

She awakened before dawn, and after a shower she headed into the kitchen to start the coffee and think about what the men might want for breakfast.

As she got out the ingredients to make waffles, she consciously shoved thoughts of Gabriel from her head. When the coffee had finished brewing, she poured herself a cup and stood at the kitchen window, watching the sun peek over the horizon.

There was no sign of the storm that had passed in the middle of the night, just like she knew not to expect Gabriel to even acknowledge that anything had happened between them, either.

As she sipped the strong brew, her thoughts turned to the people who were missing from the house. She was losing faith in anyone finding them alive, and that lack of faith horrified her.

Like the men working the case, a deep frustration welled up inside her. Who could have taken the Connellys? Why had they been taken?

And when was it time for her and Cory to leave here? There was a part of her that wanted to flee the pain of being here, where shadows of the missing danced in every corner, yet there was also a part of her that felt anchored here. She felt like a caretaker who had been given the responsibility for maintaining this place until Daniella returned.

With each long day that passed, she had a terrible feeling deep in her heart that Daniella was never coming back. She left the window and sat at the table, the last place the family had been before their disappearance.

She looked up in surprise as Andrew walked into the kitchen carrying a cup of coffee from the pot in the dining room. "You're an early bird this morning," she said.

He grinned and joined her at the table. "I went to bed early last night and slept deep and hard." He took a sip of his coffee, leaned back in the chair and looked out the window. "It's so peaceful here. It's hard to believe that anything bad ever happened."

"It's getting more and more difficult for me to hold on to my faith that they'll be returned safe and sound," she replied, the ache in her heart audible in the softness of her voice.

Andrew gazed at her, his brown eyes soft with sympathy. "I think missing persons cases are the worst. It's like a state of limbo that never ends. Even if they're gone for good, it would be nice if we could find them and give everyone who loved them a sense of closure."

"I'd rather get my closure by you all finding them alive," she said.

He nodded. "That's what we'd all like to happen." He frowned thoughtfully. "But I have to be truthful with you—the statistics are working against us with every day that passes and they aren't found."

"I know," she replied somberly. "I'm making waffles for breakfast this morning," she said, needing a change of topic. "Do you want me to go ahead and whip up some now, or should we wait until your partners are up and around?" she asked.

"Jackson was in the shower when I left the room. Who knows when Gabriel will be up. He went into town late last night for some alone time and a few beers. Thank the Lord he isn't the type to get drunk and do anything stupid," he said with a wry grin. "That man is definitely all work and no play."

Marlena jumped up from the table. "I'll go ahead and get started on the waffles," she said.

Special Agent Gabriel Blankenship was all work and no play, except for last night in a dream that she knew she'd never forget.

GABRIEL WAS IN a foul mood. At the moment he, Andrew and Jackson were headed toward a storage facility where the owner of the property had indicated one of the units was emitting the smell of decomposition.

But that wasn't what had him in a foul mood. It was Marlena. Last night, he'd thought that he'd rid himself of whatever it was about her that had him itching with the need to possess her. He'd thought that by taking her he'd be rid of her, that she'd be completely out of his mind.

The moment he saw her this morning, he knew he'd been wrong. Just watching her serve them waffles had reset what felt like a ticking time bomb inside him.

Although he'd barely acknowledged her presence, somehow he'd noticed that her peach-colored sundress was cinched at her slender waist, her sandals were gold and she smelled like a bouquet of fresh flowers.

He now clenched the steering wheel tight, trying to

erase the night before from his mind. She'd been more than he'd expected, and he had trouble forgetting the taste of her, the feel of her silky flesh against his.

"I sure hope this is a wild goose chase," Jackson said, pulling Gabriel from thoughts of Marlena. "The last thing I want to find is that family rotting away in some storage unit."

"That makes three of us," Andrew said from the backseat. "I feel bad for Marlena. I was having a cup of coffee with her this morning before the two of you got up and we were talking about how these kinds of cases put the people left behind in limbo. As much as I'd hate to find the Connellys dead, at least that would be some closure for the people at the bed-and-breakfast."

"We all know they're probably dead by now," Jackson said matter-of-factly. "It's been almost two weeks since they disappeared. There has been no ransom demand to give reason for belief that anyone wants to keep them alive."

"Yeah, but the problem is we haven't been able to find anyone who might want them dead," Gabriel replied. Although he, too, believed that the family was dead, he wasn't willing to give up all hope just yet.

The vehicle was filled with the stale air of frustration that had ridden with them each time they headed into the small town of Bachelor Moon.

Gabriel had utilized all the tools he had at his disposal to check into Sam's and Daniella's backgrounds, to see if a red flag would pop up, but there was nothing. He'd checked with Sam's director at the Kansas City field office to see if Sam had worked any cases that might have come back to haunt him, but the odds of that were slim considering Sam had been gone from the agency for over two years.

He'd called his own director this morning to check in and to admit that they still had no clues, no trail, no way to advance the investigation. He'd been hoping that they'd be pulled off the case, that he'd be forced to leave Bachelor Moon and the temptation of Marlena Meyers behind, but that hadn't happened.

He'd been instructed to give it more time and continue to seek answers. Gabriel knew he had to forget his preoccupation with Marlena and get back to focusing solely on solving this mystery.

The storage yard was on the west side of the small town, and as Gabriel pulled up to the tiny building that served as the office, he had a bad feeling in his gut.

If they found the family dead in one of these tinbox units, he could only hope that the perp had left behind some kind of evidence that they could use to hunt him down.

If the family had been killed, Gabriel would not only want to find the killer, but he'd also like to know why they were killed. Motives always intrigued him. As far as he was concerned, the intents of criminals were almost as fascinating as the criminals themselves.

The work was what was important to him, and nothing more. Women came and went, and love was a make-believe emotion that sold Valentine's Day cards and flowers but had nothing to do with his world.

The three of them got out of the car and were met by the manager, a tall, thin older man who introduced himself as Burt Buchannan. "I'm normally not here on Sundays, but I decided after church to come in this afternoon and do a little lawn work. I was weed eating around some of the units this morning and noticed the smell." His long nose wrinkled up as if recalling the foul odor. "I figured you all would want to know who rents it, so I looked it up in my records, and for the past four years, it's been rented by a Carl Gifford."

"We appreciate you calling us so quickly," Andrew said. "We'll try not to take up too much of your time."

Burt shrugged. "Got nobody at home waiting for me. My wife passed three years ago."

"Sorry to hear that. Do you know Mr. Gifford?" Gabriel asked.

Burt shook his head. "I've been working here for over ten years. I had to have met him once when he came in to rent the unit, but I have no real memory of it, and I don't think I've seen him since."

"How does he pay his monthly bill?" Jackson asked.

"It's an automatic draft from his bank account, so he never has to come into the office." Burt gestured toward the official entrance to the storage units. "Everyone who rents a unit gets an electronic card that they swipe, and it opens the gate so people can access their units at all times of the day or night."

"Do you have keys to all the units?" Jackson asked.

Burt nodded. "It's part of the rental agreement that I have a duplicate key to all the units, and no other locks are allowed. You wouldn't believe how many people don't pay after the first month or two and leave me with a shed full of crap locked up that has to be taken away." He pulled a ring filled with keys from his pocket.

"Let's take a look at the unit in question," Gabriel said with a hint of impatience. The sun was hot, he was irritable, and he just wanted to know if the family was here or not. He wanted to solve this case and get the heck out of Dodge.

He needed to be back in Baton Rouge, where meals came from the closest fast-food restaurant or from a can, not served by a sexy woman he couldn't get out of his mind. He wanted his own bed, not the one where he could tell she'd plumped his pillow and pulled up his sheets, because the scent of her was everywhere in the room.

He followed the rest of them through a maze of metal buildings with painted numbers on each one and wondered what was hidden behind the doors, trying to stay focused on the here and now.

They stopped in front of unit 2137. "This is it," Burt said. "If you walk around the back, you can really smell it."

The three agents walked to the rear entrance of the unit where half the weeds had been cut down, and the smell instantly hit Gabriel.

"Oh, wow," Andrew said, and took several steps back from the building as his face turned a faint shade of green.

Andrew had the biggest appetite and the weakest stomach of anyone Gabriel had ever worked with. He grinned as Andrew worked to keep down the big lunch he'd eaten.

The smell of decomposition was one you never forgot and would never mistake for anything else. It had a distinctive odor all its own.

"Something is definitely dead in there," Jackson

drawled. "And whatever it is, it's been dead for a while."

"I doubt that. Decomposition would have happened pretty fast in this tin box in this kind of heat," Gabriel replied. It would be tragic if they opened the unit only to discover that the family had been killed just a day or so earlier.

They walked back around to the front where Burt awaited them. "Open it," Gabriel said, mentally preparing himself for the worst.

Burt fumbled with the keys, seeming to take forever to finally find the right one. He bent down and unlocked the padlock, removed it and then pulled up the garage-style door.

A thick cloud of black flies flew out as the afternoon sunshine filled the inside. The smell was nearly overwhelming, and as Jackson and Gabriel moved forward, Andrew and Burt stepped back.

For a moment Gabriel and Jackson remained frozen in place.

"Sweet Jesus," Jackson finally whispered.

Gabriel stared at the three blood-covered canvases on the concrete floor, each covering something big enough to be a body. His heart dropped to the pit of his stomach.

He'd hoped it wouldn't end like this. He didn't realize until this moment how badly he'd wanted to find the Connellys alive, not just for them, not just for himself but for Marlena, as well.

"Go get some gloves and booties," he said to Andrew.

Andrew ran back to the car to retrieve what was

required. Gabriel looked at the rest of the interior of the unit, seeking something that might aid them in an investigation.

They had one thing in their favor. Even if the name Burt had been given by whomever had rented this place was false, they could follow the money back to the source.

"Why would a criminal who's been smart enough not to leave a single clue behind be stupid enough to use an automatic withdrawal from his bank account to pay for this place?" Jackson asked, his thoughts mirroring Gabriel's.

"Maybe he figured nobody would ever know the bodies were here. Maybe he was just stupid enough not to realize that Burt might smell something funny out here."

"Looks like the only thing in here is whatever is under those canvases and that big dolly." Jackson pointed to a red dolly standing in a far corner. It had probably been used to cart the bodies into the storage unit.

By that time Andrew was back. Both Gabriel and Jackson put on the booties and gloves, and then advanced on the first bloody canvas.

Gabriel had seen a lot of horrible things in his years as an FBI agent, and he'd been desensitized up to a point, but as he approached the corner of the first canvas to see what lay beneath, he prayed the first thing he saw wasn't little Macy's face staring sightlessly in death back at him.

He exchanged a glance with Jackson, who he knew

had to be feeling the same emotions that now roiled through him: dread, disappointment and, finally, failure.

He grabbed the canvas, drew a deep breath and then yanked it back. All the air in his lungs whooshed out of him as he stared at what lay beneath.

"What in the hell?" Jackson's voice rang out with anger as the two of them stared at the big dead, decomposing alligator beneath the canvas.

An overwhelming rage welled up inside Gabriel as he stalked over to the other two forms and threw back the canvases to expose two more decaying alligators.

"Call Sheriff Thompson," he said to Burt. "Tell him he's got a situation out here that needs to be resolved. This isn't our problem."

Gabriel stepped out of the unit, pulled off his gloves and booties and stalked toward the car, aware of Jackson and Andrew hurrying after him.

Chapter Eight

That evening Marlena found Gabriel seated on the sofa in the great room, the television turned on, but the volume so low it couldn't be heard.

He was half sprawled on the sofa, fingers rubbing back and forth in the center of his forehead. She'd heard about the alligator event and knew that it had been a particularly difficult day for the three agents.

"Headache?" she asked sympathetically as she walked into the room.

"A killer," he admitted.

"Can I get you something?"

"It's just stress. Eventually it will go away." There was pain in the sound of his deep voice.

"Sometimes a really good massage helps." She moved around the sofa to stand behind him and placed her fingers on his temples. "May I?" she asked.

He dropped his hand to his lap. "Knock yourself out."

She moved her fingers lightly at his temples and then began to massage with more force, working across his forehead and then back and around to the base of his skull. His thick, soft hair felt good beneath her fingers, but her desire was strictly focused on easing his pain.

He began to relax, his shoulders losing their tenseness, his neck moving more freely with her instead of fighting her.

She didn't know how long she had massaged Gabriel's head before Andrew came downstairs. "Hey, I could use one of those," he said.

Gabriel stiffened and sat up straighter. She dropped her hands from his head. "Do you have a headache, too?" she asked.

Andrew cast her one of his easygoing smiles. "Nah. I'll settle for leftover apple pie from dinner."

"In the refrigerator. Feel free to help yourself," she replied as she walked around the sofa and sat on the opposite end from Gabriel.

"Better?" she asked the moment Andrew disappeared from the room.

"Actually, it is a little better. Thank you, but you didn't have to do that." His dark blue eyes gazed at her with weariness.

"You were in pain. I wanted to do whatever I could to ease that pain," she countered.

"Is that because of what happened between us the other night?" His gaze was wary.

"I don't know what you're talking about. I had an amazing dream the other night, and then I woke up." She frowned at him, wondering what was going on in his head. "Gabriel, don't read anything into it. I was just trying to be nice to you."

He stared at the far wall for a long moment and

then looked back at her. "I'm not used to people being nice," he replied.

"Then you've been running around with the wrong kind of people," she observed. Sensing that he wanted to be alone, that further conversation would only make him more wary, she told him good-night and then went into the kitchen to sit with Andrew for a few minutes at the small kitchen table before turning in for the night.

"Tough day," she said.

Andrew dug a fork into an oversize piece of the left-over pie she'd made that day. "The worst. We were sure that those canvases covered the bodies of your friends. None of us wanted to come back here and tell you that we'd found them in that storage unit." He paused to shovel a large bite into his mouth and washed it down with a sip of milk.

"You like him," he said.

"Who?" she asked, although she knew exactly who he was talking about.

"Gabriel. The air practically snaps when the two of you are in the same room." He eyed her sympathetically. "Just a little word of warning. I've been partners with Gabriel for a couple of years now. He's a tough nut to crack, and he doesn't do love. I wouldn't want you to get hurt."

"Trust me, I know exactly what kind of person Gabriel is. You don't have to worry about me," she said, warmed by his attempt to let her know Gabriel wasn't a man looking for a future with any woman. "What about you? Do you have a girlfriend or wife back in Baton Rouge?"

"Girlfriend, soon to be fiancée," he replied, his eyes

lighting as if merely mentioning her caused his heart to soar. "Her name is Suzi, and she's the love of my life. We've been together for two years, and I'm just about ready to put a ring on her."

"That's nice. She's a lucky woman," she replied and then got up from the table. "And thanks for the warning about my own love life, but it was completely unnecessary. I have no illusions about anything, and now I think I'll say good-night. Just put your dishes in the sink when you're finished."

"Good night, Marlena, and thanks for taking such good care of us."

"My pleasure," she replied and then went into her private quarters.

Minutes later, as she got into bed, her thoughts naturally drifted to Gabriel. Despite Andrew's warnings, and what Gabriel had told her himself, she could love him if he'd let her, if she allowed herself to.

But she couldn't, and tomorrow she intended to ask him if it would be okay for her and Cory to move on, to leave Bachelor Moon and the bed-and-breakfast and begin their new lives. She'd already told Cory to prepare to leave, that their time line had been moved up by the Connellys' disappearance.

She wasn't sure what would happen to the bed-and-breakfast if she left. She assumed Pamela would step in to manage the business until something broke with the case.

Marlena awoke early as usual the next morning, and as she sipped her coffee, she made a list of things she'd need to do to transition from this place that had felt like home for the better part of the past two years to a new city, a new location to start over.

Although she knew Cory would hate to leave here, she also knew he'd do well with the move. He was a friendly kid and would make a circle of friends easily, especially once he was enrolled in a trade school.

She had enough money tucked away to pay for a year of college tuition for herself, and she knew that Cory had enough money in savings to pay for trade school. She could get a job waitressing to pay their living expenses, and life would go on.

Without Daniella. Without Macy and Sam. Her heart ached with their absence, but if there was one thing Marlena had learned over the years, it was that she couldn't control fate and could only deal with the consequences of her own actions and whatever fate cast her way.

Fate had taken away Sam and Daniella and their little girl, and after this much time, deep in her heart she didn't believe they were ever returning.

She stopped her list making to fix breakfast for the men, who were quiet and somber. Even Andrew appeared subdued as he ate his usual big breakfast.

Gabriel barely met her gaze, appearing distracted as he ate quickly and then waited on the front porch for the other two to join him.

Once they had left, Cory and John appeared at the back door looking for breakfast, as well. She fed them bacon and eggs, and then watched at the window as they left the house to get to work in the yard.

With breakfast taken care of, and assuming the men wouldn't be home for lunch, she pulled some thick steaks out of the freezer and washed potatoes for baking for dinner that evening.

By that time Pamela had arrived to do the Monday cleaning. Marlena went into her own quarters to stay out of Pamela's way. There she did a little cleaning of her own, pulling out the dusty old suitcase that she'd brought with her to Bachelor Moon from Chicago and opening it in the storage area to eventually begin to pack.

Pamela worked until one o'clock and then left, her chores taking less time since the only guests were the three men. Once she was gone, Marlena was surprised and a bit dismayed when a knock came at the door, and she looked out to see Thomas Brady on the porch.

"I've been thinking about you all week," he said as she let him inside and gestured him toward the sofa in the great room. "How are you holding up?"

"As well as I can." She sat on the far side of the sofa from him, aware that the agents hadn't yet cleared him off their persons of interest list.

"Is there anything I can do? You must be worried sick about Sam and Daniella and little Macy."

"I am worried," she replied.

"You know I'm here for you whenever you need me, Marlena." His gaze was soft and caring. "I just don't know how to help you through this difficult time."

Even though she felt no personal fear of him, she couldn't help but notice again how much at ease he seemed without Sam and Daniella's presence in the house. His arm was flung across the back of the sofa as if he owned it, and he appeared completely relaxed.

"Maybe what you need is a nice dinner out. Surely

you aren't responsible for feeding the FBI agents seven nights a week. How about this Friday you take some time off for yourself and let me take you out and wine and dine you?"

Marlena realized it was past time to put an end to this romance that never was. "Thomas, I've appreciated your friendship over the past year, but my feelings for you are always just going to be as a friend, nothing romantic."

"Ouch." His smile crumbled and his brown eyes darkened. He pulled his arm from the back of the sofa and leaned toward her. "Are you sure with more time the friendship wouldn't develop into something romantic? Because I have to tell you the truth, Marlena. I definitely feel very romantic feelings toward you, and I have since the moment we met."

"I'm sorry," Marlena replied, truly meaning it. She knew all about unrequited love, about the pain of rejection, but she also knew she couldn't allow Thomas to go on pretending that they were in any way involved in a romantic relationship.

"This isn't something that's going to build into a romance with more time," she replied. "Besides, if the FBI allows it, I intend to move away from here in the next week or so. I'm sorry, Thomas, but you deserve to find a wonderful woman who will love you with all her heart. I'm just not her."

"I knew it," he finally replied. "I knew you didn't feel the same for me as I did for you. I feel it when we're together, but I had hoped with more time it would change." He shrugged and stood. "This place won't be the same without you and Cory around, but I guess I'll be leaving you alone now."

Hc walked toward the door, and when he reached it, he turned back to look at her. "I hope you have a great life, Marlena. Wherever you go, whomever you wind up with, I wish you only happiness."

"And the same for you," she replied.

She remained on the sofa for a few minutes after he'd gone. Life might have been easier if she'd fallen head over heels in love with Thomas. She believed he was a good man, and found it hard to believe that he might have had anything to do with whatever had happened to the Connelly family. Thomas was a hard worker who lived in a nice ranch house that had more than enough room for a wife and a brother-in-law young enough to be considered a stepson.

Cory could have remained here, working with John. She would have been able to maintain the friendships she'd made in Bachelor Moon, and she knew Thomas was a man who would have been satisfied with her being a homemaker and mother.

But instead she found herself precariously close to loving a man who would never love her back, a man she'd already had steamy-hot sex with and a man who would probably never think of her again once they parted ways.

She could only hope that the beginning of finding true happiness and love was just around the corner, that starting fresh with new purpose and drive would bring different things and exciting people into her life.

Nobody could be as exciting as Gabriel, a little voice

whispered in her head. Nobody will ever match the way he loved your body, that voice taunted.

"Shut up," she said aloud, and got off the sofa, deciding that maybe she'd cut some fresh flowers for bouquets for the house.

The late afternoon air was hot and humid as she walked down to the gardening shed, and grabbed a wicker basket and cutting shears. She schooled her mind to blankness as she went about the pleasure of picking out the most colorful blooms that would make the prettiest bouquets.

Daniella had loved to keep the house filled with fresh flowers, and John kept the flower beds blooming throughout the heat of the summer.

By the time she had her basket full, it was almost three o'clock. She put the shears back in the shed and then hurried into the house, hoping to get the bouquets made before it was time to start supper preparations.

As she worked on arrangements, not only for the center of the dining room table but also smaller ones for the bedrooms where the men slept, she found her thoughts drifting to Gabriel.

He'd given her just enough of a peek into his childhood to understand how he felt about love and about loving. She got it, and yet she had responded to her own mother's abandonment by wanting love more than ever. She and Gabriel were flip sides of the same coin.

She would guess that they both suffered abandonment issues, but they had responded in diametrically opposite ways. She could only hope that someday in the future he would discover the desire to love and be loved. Maybe someday a very special woman would be able to break through the shield he'd erected to keep himself from any more pain when it came to love.

It hurt her more than she expected to know that she wasn't that woman. It surprised her to realize how badly she wished she could be that woman for him.

Carrying the two smaller arrangements of flowers up the stairs, she decided to place the one with sweet peas in Gabriel's room. The heady scent of the blooms might please him. He wouldn't know that she'd specifically chosen the prettiest of the arrangements for his room.

Once she'd delivered the flowers, she started down the stairs, but paused on the first step as she heard a noise from someplace behind her.

Before she could turn, before she could consciously assess what kind of sound it had been, hands shoved her back. Just like the night at the pond, she had a moment of weightlessness, only this time there wasn't a dark pond to fall into—there were thirteen steps that in the span of an instant she knew she was going to hit.

GABRIEL, ANDREW AND Jackson stood in Sheriff Thompson's small office as he filled them in on the details of the debacle in the storage unit with the dead gators.

Thompson sat back in his leather chair behind his desk and scratched his protruding belly, then leaned forward with a deep frown cutting across his broad forehead.

"Carl Gifford is a stinking slimy swamp rat whom I've suspected of illegally poaching for years. That storage unit and the banking records finally confirmed it." Thompson shook his head and uttered a small laugh.

"Only an idiot would put his illegal goods in a storage unit paid for every month out of his own bank account."

"I'm sure he never expected anyone else to open up the door to that unit. Where is he now?" Gabriel asked, his stomach knotting as he thought of those first moments staring at the bloody canvases.

"He's been in my custody for the past two nights. Got himself drunk and stupid and assaulted one of my deputies, so I locked him up. Apparently the gators were supposed to be sold to another party the night that I threw him behind bars. He'll be in my jail for a while since I've got all I need now to add the additional charge of poaching."

"So the mystery of the alligators has been solved," Jackson said.

"But it moves us no further in our own investigation," Gabriel added in frustration.

"I wish I could be more help to you all, but I just don't have anything else to give you," Thompson said.

"We appreciate you calling us in to let us know about the gators. It was the damnedest thing I've ever seen," Jackson said, and shook his head in disbelief.

"Let's get out of here," Gabriel said. "I think it's time we call it a day." He thanked the sheriff, and then the three of them headed for their car.

It had been another fruitless day of interviews and walking the streets, and Gabriel was ready to get back to the bed-and-breakfast, out of the heat and humidity.

He was tired. It was the bone weariness of failure, a weight he wasn't accustomed to carrying. He was supposed to be leading this team investigation, and he'd never felt more helpless.

He was out of ideas and out of energy. At the moment the only place he could lead his team was back to the B and B where they would talk over the facts they didn't have, eat without appetites—except for maybe Andrew—and dream about the family they couldn't find.

They rode home in silence, the kind of silence that filled the interior of the car like a pool of stagnant water. Gabriel breathed a deep sigh as he pulled in front of the house. It was early, just before four in the afternoon, but as far as he was concerned, their day was done.

Gabriel was the first one through the door, and he froze at the sight of Marlena sprawled face down on the floor at the foot of the stairs.

Although his heart remained stopped, he raced to her side, relieved to see that she was conscious, but scared to death as he crouched down next to her.

"I fell," she said, and tears began to course from her eyes.

"From where?" he asked as Jackson and Andrew joined him by her side.

"From the top stair."

"Call for an ambulance," Gabriel said urgently. His heart banged painfully against his ribs. Who knew how many bones she might have broken? What kind of internal damage she must be suffering?

"No, I think I'm okay. I've just been afraid to move without anyone here in case I'm not all right." Despite her words, her voice was filled with a pain that rattled through his bones.

"Make the call," Gabriel said.

"Really, I don't think anything is broken." Her green eyes held a wealth of emotion as she gazed at Gabriel. "Just help me sit up and I'll be fine." With a deep moan, she rolled over from her stomach to her back.

Gabriel held up a hand to halt the call Jackson had been about to make, and then he took Marlena's hands in his and pulled her to a sitting position.

"Anything feel broken? Can you move your legs?" Her face was bleached of color, and she winced with the movement. Gabriel didn't release her hands as his heart pounded a million beats a minute. The tightness in his chest eased a little as she managed to move both of her legs.

"I don't think anything is broken. Just help me up off the floor," she said, her gaze never leaving his. It was as if she were tapping into his strength. She didn't realize how little he had. She couldn't know that the sight of her unmoving on the floor had sapped all his energy and had weakened his knees.

He stood and pulled her up. She got to her feet and instantly leaned against his chest, deep sobs escaping her as he ran his hands down the length of her back to assure himself he felt nothing broken.

"I'm taking you to the emergency room," he said as he stared up the staircase that suddenly appeared horrifyingly steep and endless. If she'd fallen from the top, she was lucky she wasn't dead. "You need to be thoroughly checked out by a doctor."

With his decision made, he gently lifted her up in his arms, terrified that he might hurt her more than she already was, yet needing to get her to the hospital as quickly as possible. Andrew opened the front door and then hurried ahead of them to open the passenger side of the car, too.

Gabriel eased her down onto the seat as gently as possible, then went to get behind the wheel. "We'll be back after she's been examined from head to toe." Andrew nodded and stepped away from the car.

Gabriel shot out of the bed-and-breakfast entrance and headed to the small hospital he'd seen in Bachelor Moon. "How long had you been lying there?" he asked, his heart tied in a painful knot as he thought of her on the floor, all alone and hurting.

"Not too long. I never lost consciousness or anything. I tucked and rolled. When I knew I was falling, all I could think about was, if my head hit a stair, I would probably die." She raised her hand to her face and began to quietly weep again.

Gabriel didn't know if it was emotional wounds or physical ones that kept her crying. All he knew was that he needed to get her to the hospital as quickly as possible.

They didn't speak again, and when he pulled in front of the emergency room door, he got out of the car and yelled for assistance. Shock might have allowed her to move, allowed him to pick her up in his arms without her even knowing that she had broken bones or internal injuries. He wasn't about to let her walk in on her own without knowing more about her current condition.

It took only minutes for her to be loaded onto a gurney and whisked away. Gabriel was led to a waiting room where he sank down and worried a shaky hand through his hair.

For just an instant when he'd seen her on the floor,

he'd thought she was dead, and his heart had plummeted with a sharp grief he'd never known before in his life.

And in that instant, he'd recognized that he did care about her. He didn't want to—he had no intention of allowing her any deeper into his heart—but he had to acknowledge that she'd made a little headway where nobody else ever had before.

He jumped as his cell phone rang. He pulled it from his pocket to see Jackson's number. "Hey," he answered.

"We just wanted to let you know that she appeared to be alone in the house when she fell, and we didn't find anything on the stairs that might have made her fall."

"Thanks. I didn't notice what kind of shoes she was wearing. Maybe she just got tripped up in her own feet," Gabriel replied. "We'll know within a couple of hours. She's in with the doctor now, and I imagine they'll want to x-ray every part of her body."

"I hope she's okay. We'll just see you when we see you," Jackson replied.

"One more thing," Gabriel said. "If you see Cory around, you might want to tell him what happened."

"Will do."

Gabriel disconnected and placed his phone in his pocket, then leaned back in his chair and closed his eyes. She could have died. The mere thought increased the beat of his heart.

Thank God she'd been smart. She'd tucked and rolled when most people made the mistake of trying to break their fall and in the process broke bones in their arms or legs, or their necks.

She'd been smart, and she'd been lucky. He just hoped the doctor didn't find something that contradicted that belief. He didn't want her hurt. He didn't want her in pain.

He remembered how she'd massaged his head when he'd had a simple headache, her fingers firm and yet so caring as she'd attempted to work his misery away.

He hadn't been sitting in the waiting room long when Cory came flying in the door, his eyes wild with fear.

"Is she okay?" He started for the door to the examining rooms, but Gabriel stopped him.

"Cory, sit here." He patted the place next to him. "She should be fine. We just need to wait for the doctor to let us know for sure."

Cory sank down, bringing with him the scent of the outdoors, a faint hint of sweat and the unmistakable odor of marijuana.

"Jackson said she fell down the stairs. She could have died." His blue-green eyes looked at Gabriel and filled with a mist of tears. "She's all I've got. If anything happened to her, I don't know what I'd do."

Gabriel clapped the young man on the shoulder. "She's going to be just fine, Cory. She managed to get up, and nothing appeared to be broken."

"But if she hit her head, she could have brain bleeding or something. John told me that's what happened to his mother. She fell down some stairs, and everyone thought she was fine until they found out her brain was bleeding."

"I'm sure the doctor will check Marlena all over," Gabriel assured the young man.

Cory released a deep sigh and dropped his head to his hands, as if silently praying. Gabriel gave him a few minutes of silence.

"Does your sister know you're smoking pot?" Gabriel finally asked softly.

Cory's head shot up and his eyes widened. "What are you talking about?" he replied.

"Come on, Cory. I've been around a long time, and I can smell it on you. Don't try to fool me."

"I just smoke it sometimes," Cory replied defensively. "I got freaked out when I heard about my sister, so I took a few puffs on the way here. Are you going to turn me in to the sheriff?" he asked fearfully.

"No."

"Are you going to narc me out to my sister?"

"I think she has enough on her mind right now, but I'm sure Marlena isn't stupid, either. Smoking dope isn't going to get you anywhere, Cory."

"I know. John has told me the same thing."

"Then you should listen." Gabriel sat back in his seat, deciding enough had been said on the topic. As far as he could tell, Cory was a good kid and hopefully he'd make good choices in his life, but he wasn't Gabriel's problem.

It felt as if they had waited for hours. The two men took turns pacing up and down the length of the waiting room. The longer it took, the more worried Gabriel became. Should he have called for an ambulance? Had he hurt her by moving her? By lifting her up and carrying her?

The memory of the sound of her weeping resonated through him, bringing with it an ache that refused to vanish. He couldn't remember the last time any woman's tears had moved him. Yet hers had.

He didn't want to think about the reason for this anomaly. He didn't want to pull out whatever emotions he felt for Marlena and examine them. He told himself he'd be as worried, as frightened for any person who'd been a caretaker for him and his team for almost two weeks.

Both Cory and Gabriel jumped out of their chairs as a white-coated doctor approached them. "I'm Dr. Frank Sheldon, and Marlena is one lucky woman. I found no broken bones, no head injury and no reason to keep her here. She's free to go as soon as she gets dressed."

Gabriel wasn't sure who released the biggest sigh of relief, him or Marlena's brother.

"I need to warn you that she's badly bruised, and I expect by tomorrow she's going to feel pain in places she didn't know she had body parts. What she needs most is bed rest for a couple of days. I've written her a prescription for pain medication, and it can be filled here at the hospital pharmacy. She should go home, take a couple of pills and go directly to bed," Dr. Sheldon said.

"We'll take good care of her," Gabriel replied.

The object of their conversation came through the swinging doors that led to the emergency units, shuffling like an old woman even as a forced smile curved her lips.

"Cory, why don't you sit here with her while I get her prescription filled?" Gabriel suggested. There was no way he wanted her walking any farther than she needed to.

"Works for me," Marlena said as she eased down on the waiting room sofa with an agony-filled sigh. Cory immediately sat next to her, and as Gabriel took the prescription from her and left to hunt down the pharmacy, Marlena was assuring Cory that she'd be fine.

Gabriel followed the signs that led him to the pharmacy, and within minutes he had the pill bottle in hand and was hurrying back to where he was surprised to find Marlena sitting alone.

"What happened to Cory?"

"I sent him home." She stood, the simple action obviously painful as she winced. "There was no point in him hanging around here. There's nothing he can do to help me."

"Should I get a wheelchair to take you out?" he asked with concern.

"No, I'll be fine. Let's just get out of here." She took baby steps toward the exit, and Gabriel walked at her side, a hand under her elbow, afraid that she might fall at any moment.

He didn't breathe a sigh of relief until she was back in the passenger seat, her seat belt around her waist. "You're going straight to bed," he said once he was behind the wheel.

"But I had steaks laid out to cook for dinner," she protested weakly.

"Andrew will know what to do with the steaks. You are to go home, take a couple of these pills and not worry about anything else. The doctor said you need a couple of days of bed rest, and that's what's going to happen."

She nodded as if too sore, too weak to argue. "I sent Cory on home so that I could talk to you in private before we get back to the bed-and-breakfast."

He tensed, wondering if she was going to bring up the night they'd shared, a night that had haunted him ever since—but a night he refused to dwell on.

"Talk in private about what?" he asked. He glanced over and met her gaze. In the depths of her wide green eyes, he saw something more than pain.

He saw fear.

"I didn't accidentally fall down those stairs. I was on the top step when I thought I heard something behind me, and that's when I was pushed."

Chapter Nine

Marlena awakened to pain. Her shoulders hurt, her hips ached and her ribs screamed in harmony. Even her eyelids protested, and for several long minutes she remained unmoving in her bed, trying to decide if she wanted to open her eyes and face a new day or not.

She'd been awake late despite taking two of the pain pills. After telling Gabriel she'd been pushed down the stairs, he'd given her the pills, waited for her to change into her nightgown then tucked her into bed and left her quarters.

Although she'd been groggy and half out of it, he'd checked back in with her a bit later to let her know that the door that led to the old servant stairs had been unlocked and the door that led out of the basement had been open, as if somebody had exited in a hurry.

It was an easy guess that whoever had pushed her had crept through the basement door, up the stairs and then waited for the opportunity to shove her.

It had been attempted murder, and now there was no doubt in her mind that the night by the pond she had been shoved into the water, as well. Two attempts on her life.

This thought was enough for her to finally open her

eyes and ease up to a half-prone position against her pillows. Her heart beat an uneven rhythm. Who would want her dead? Why would somebody be after her? She had nothing. She hadn't had any problems with anyone. Was this somehow tied to the disappearance of Sam, Daniella and Macy? But how? And why?

Just thinking about all of it made her head ache. She smelled coffee and the lingering scent of bacon and glanced at her bedside clock, shocked to see that it was after eight. She couldn't remember the last time she'd slept so late.

She sat up straighter as Gabriel appeared in her doorway carrying one of the TV trays that were kept for guest use in the great room.

"Good morning," he said.

"Right now it's not feeling so good," she replied.

He flashed her a grin, and the warmth of that quick gesture seemed to magically ease some of the aches and pains inside her. "I thought you might like some coffee and a little breakfast. You're supposed to take your pain pills on a full stomach."

He placed the tray next to her bed and then sat in the chair nearby. "Eat," he commanded.

With effort, she moved to a full sitting position, and the first thing she reached for was the cup of coffee. She took a sip and eyed him over the rim. "You didn't have to do this for me."

"I can't take credit for the bacon and eggs. That was Andrew's talent. But I did make the toast and fix your coffee on the tray to present to you."

"And a fine presentation it is," she replied. She picked up a piece of the toast and took a bite, then chased it with another swallow of coffee while he continued to gaze at her. "I don't suppose you found footsteps or fingerprints in the basement or on the door upstairs that would help you catch a bad guy."

He frowned. "Of course not. That would make it all too easy."

She frowned and realized that even her forehead hurt. "Do you think this is all somehow tied to whatever happened to Sam and Daniella?"

He hesitated a moment and then sighed. "I don't know, Marlena. Eat first, and then I've got some questions to ask you. But eat now—there's nothing worse than cold eggs."

Dutifully, she picked up her fork but only ate about half of the food on her plate and then proclaimed herself finished.

"Now take your pills."

"Not yet," she replied. "They make me really groggy, and you said you had some questions for me."

"Let me take the tray out of here first." He placed her coffee cup on the end table next to the bed and then carried the tray away. When he returned, he sat on the edge of her bed.

She was unaware that her nightgown had slipped from her shoulder until she saw him gaze there and curse beneath his breath. Her shoulder was badly bruised and in a variety of shades of deep purple.

"I'm sorry, Marlena."

She was surprised by the wealth of emotion in his voice, emotion she hadn't believed him capable of feeling.

"I'm so damned sorry."

"It's not your fault," she protested and reached out to cover one of his hands with hers.

He turned his hand over and grabbed hers. "I just feel so damned helpless. We have a missing family, and now somebody has tried to hurt you not once but twice, and I can't get a handle on any of it."

"The good thing is that both attempts on my life have been unsuccessful," she said.

He squeezed her hand. "And I'm going to do everything in my power to make sure there isn't a third. Last night the three of us decided the best way to approach everything that's happened is that Andrew and Jackson are going to continue to look for leads concerning the disappearance of the Connellys, and I'm going to focus on the threats against you." He released her hand and sat back.

She immediately missed the warmth, the security of his hand around hers. "So how do you do that?"

"I need to learn more about you, about where you came from. If you can't think of anyone from Bachelor Moon who might want to hurt you, then maybe somebody followed you from your past. Tell me about your recent life before returning here."

She hated to tell him. She hated to admit how stupid she'd been during the time she'd been in Chicago, especially the past two years there. But she knew she had to be truthful with him, even though she didn't believe she'd brought any danger with her by moving here.

"The first few years we were there, it was all about survival. I was a twenty-one-year-old with a fourteen-year-old in tow. We rented a small apartment, I got a job as a waitress at a fairly nice restaurant and Cory went to school. When I was working, I had a neighbor lady who watched Cory for me, even though he insisted he was old enough to watch himself. I knew he was an at-risk kid, with no father figure and just me to depend on."

"Must have been tough."

She winced as she shifted positions. "At times it was. And then I met Gary Holzman. He was an insurance salesman who came into the restaurant frequently, and we struck up a friendship. He was a nice man, a widower with two little daughters, and it wasn't long before we were dating."

"Were you in love with him?"

Marlena wondered why it mattered to him. "I was lonely, and unlike you, I was looking for love and family and a sense of security. When he asked me and Cory to move in with him, and I knew I could stay home and take care of his little girls, be there for Cory plus be a homemaker, I jumped at the chance. I cared about Gary and I enjoyed his company, but looking back on it now, no, I wasn't in love with him. I was in love with the idea of being part of a family."

She reached for her coffee cup, took another drink then continued. "I was definitely in love with the notion of being in love. I loved Gary's little girls and thought Gary would be a good role model for Cory. So for the next two years we lived together as a couple. I cooked and cleaned and cared for his children. I just assumed that eventually he'd propose to me, and we'd get married and live satisfactorily ever after."

"But he didn't."

A small, bitter laugh escaped her. "No, he didn't.

Instead he came home from work one night and out of the blue told me he thought the relationship aspect of his life was too complicated, that it was easier for him to just hire a housekeeper to keep the house and watch the girls, and he'd appreciate it if Cory and I would be gone by morning."

Marlena leaned her head back against the pillow, overwhelmed with emotion as she thought of that moment in time. She'd expected a ring, and instead she had gotten the boot. She wasn't sorry that she had never been married to Gary, but she'd been sorry that he'd wakened her to the fact that she'd just been settling with him, and in any case he certainly wasn't in love with her.

"That's when Cory and I wound up here. I was broke, numbed by the sudden change of our circumstances and unsure where else to turn."

"Is it possible that this Gary person may want to harm you?" Gabriel asked, his eyes dark and unreadable.

Marlena laughed again, and then winced and grabbed her ribs. Gabriel leaned forward and reached for her pill bottle. He shook out two and held them toward her. "Go on, you need them."

She took them with the last sip of her coffee and then continued talking. "I haven't heard a word from Gary since we left Chicago. He didn't want me with him when I left. I can't imagine why he'd want to hurt me after all this time. Or anyone from my life in Chicago following me here and wanting to hurt me after two years."

"Tell me about your day yesterday, from start to finish."

"After you all left, I cleaned up the kitchen, did my usual chores and took the steaks out of the freezer for dinner." She frowned, trying to remember even as a headache began to bang across her temples. "I made breakfast for Cory and John, and then they went back outside to work. Pamela came and cleaned for a couple of hours and then left."

"What else? What were you doing upstairs?" he asked gently.

"Flowers. I picked flowers." Already she could feel the edge easing off her pain, the whisper of drowsiness sweeping over her. "I wanted to put flowers in your rooms. I'd picked some beautiful ones for your room."

"I noticed them this morning. They're lovely," he replied. "It was a nice thing to do."

"I like to do nice things for you. I don't think people have been kind enough to you in your life." She felt the warmth that crept over her cheeks and hoped that later she could blame her frankness on the medication. "Anyway, I'd just put the flowers in the rooms and was about to come downstairs when somebody pushed me."

"And as far as you know, there was nobody else in the house."

"Nobody," she agreed. Tired. She was suddenly so tired, but then she remembered her conversation with Thomas. "Wait… Thomas was here."

"Thomas Brady?" Gabriel sat forward in his chair.

"He was here before I picked the flowers." She fought against the drowsiness, realizing what she had to tell him was important. "He came to ask me out to dinner, and I told him we didn't have any future to-gether, that I'd never be in love with him in a roman-tic way."

Gabriel rose from his chair. "And how did he take it?" His voice was deceptively calm.

"He seemed to take it very well." She tried to keep her heavy-lidded eyes open. "He said he understood that you couldn't make somebody love you if she didn't, that he'd sensed I wasn't feeling the same about him as he was about me. Surely you don't think he…" Her voice trailed off as she couldn't fight the effect of the pills any longer.

As she closed her eyes, she thought she felt the press of Gabriel's lips against her forehead, but it had to be a dream because he would never do anything like that in reality.

"ANDREW, YOU STAY here and keep an eye on Marlena. Jackson, you come with me." Gabriel had a head full of steam as he left Marlena's quarters and entered the dining room where the two other agents were seated.

He hadn't realized the sunshine Marlena had brought into his life until he saw her now, bruised and broken, and what he wanted more than anything was to find the person responsible and beat the hell out of him or her, make whoever it was feel the same kind of pain Marlena was feeling right now.

The sight of her slender shoulder and dainty freck-les hiding beneath vivid, violent purple bruises made him want to tear somebody's head off.

"Where are we going?" Jackson asked once they were in the car.

"To Thomas Brady's house. I want to find out where he was yesterday afternoon when Marlena was shoved down the stairs."

Jackson shot him a look of interest. "You think he's responsible?"

"It's possible," Gabriel replied. "Apparently he was here yesterday, and Marlena told him there would never be a romance between them. She said he took it well, but he might just be a good actor, and was angry enough to sneak back here and try to hurt her." Gabriel tightened his hands on the steering wheel. "If he did this to her, then I'll kill him."

"Whoa, partner. It sounds like you're taking this more than a little personally," Jackson said.

Gabriel felt his partner's speculative gaze on him and slowly eased the pressure his fingers had had on the steering wheel. "She's a nice woman, and she's obviously a target for some reason. I just want to get to the bottom of it, that's all."

Gabriel thought about the silky softness of her skin when he'd kissed her, skin that was now mottled and bruised, causing her enormous pain.

"Maybe I am a little personally involved," he finally admitted. "First somebody tried to drown her in the pond, and now this happens. She needs a champion."

"And you've decided you're that man?"

"Yeah, I guess I have," he replied. It didn't mean anything, he told himself. It had nothing to do with any kind of an emotional connection between them. It was his job. Besides, she'd said she wanted to do nice things for him.

Damn, but that single statement had punched him in

the gut. There had been no kindness in his childhood, and there certainly hadn't been any when he'd been out on the streets alone. Even when he'd joined the FBI, he'd found camaraderie among his fellow agents, but he hadn't known softness until now…until Marlena.

While he didn't intend to get drawn into it, he at least wanted her to be okay to go on with the life she'd planned in the big city, with a husband who adored her, and babies to hold and love.

When she'd talked briefly about her life with Gary Holzman in Chicago, he'd heard the yearning in her voice, the desire for the fairy-tale ending.

What amazed him was that, despite her painful experience with her mother, and then again with Gary, her desire for love hadn't waned. She didn't seem to fear being hurt again but rather was open to loving without restraint.

He might hunt down killers and put himself in dangerous situations, but he could admit to himself that between the two of them, she was the one with real courage.

"Even if Thomas did get angry and pushed her down the stairs, that doesn't explain Marlena's unexpected dunk in the pond," Jackson said, pulling Gabriel from his thoughts.

"No, it doesn't." Gabriel frowned. "But maybe he'd already sensed that she didn't want to date him. Maybe he's a psychopath who goes around trying to kill women he dates. Hell, I don't know what to make of it all." He slammed his palm against the steering wheel.

"I think maybe now would be a good time to take a few deep breaths," Jackson said. "Either that, or I'm going to have to slap you, because you're having some sort of a hysterical breakdown."

Gabriel drew in a long draw of oxygen and then grinned at the man in the seat next to him. "Thanks for warning me before you tried to slap me."

"You're welcome." Jackson returned his grin.

By the time they pulled up in front of Thomas's attractive two-story house, Gabriel had calmed down a bit. Jackson had reminded him that before yesterday, Thomas shouldn't have had a motive for attempting to hurt Marlena, which put the near drowning in question.

It was easy to speculate that whoever had pushed her in the pond was the same person who had shoved her down the stairs. The M.O. was the same…and it would appear somebody wanted Marlena dead, but they also wanted it to look like an accident.

"Are we getting out, or are we just going to sit in the car and meditate?" Jackson asked drily.

Gabriel shut off the engine. "We're getting out. I was gathering my thoughts."

"I'm glad one of us has some thoughts left to gather."

The two got out of the car and approached the house. They'd been here before to ask Thomas questions about the Connelly family.

While they had learned that he had, indeed, been in New Orleans during the time the family had been taken and they had in their possession copies of the receipts of his motel-room bill, Thomas was an independent contractor, so there were no copies of work hours, no coworkers to question about his schedule.

He'd never fallen off their list of persons of interest because of how close New Orleans was.

Be honest with yourself, Gabriel thought as they headed toward the front door. *He's still a person of interest on a short list of two.* Thomas Brady and the hotheaded Ryan Sherman, with his shaky alibi provided by his dopehead girlfriend, were the only two names on the list.

Gabriel knocked on the door with a firm fist. Brady's work truck was in the driveway, so Gabriel assumed the man was at home.

The door opened as Gabriel was about to knock again. Thomas Brady looked at the two FBI agents in confusion. "I thought I was done with you all. I gave you everything I had from my trip to New Orleans."

"We're here about another matter. Mind if we come in?" Gabriel kept his voice calm. In fact, he attempted to be pleasant but knew he hadn't quite made it when Thomas's brown eyes narrowed suspiciously.

"I can't imagine any other matter we'd have to discuss," he replied, not indicating any desire to allow them into his home.

"How about Marlena?"

"What about her?" There was no missing the slight softness that filled Thomas's voice or the sudden uncertainty that darkened his eyes as he looked first at Jackson and then back at Gabriel.

"She was shoved down the staircase in the bed-and-breakfast yesterday after you left," Gabriel said.

Thomas's features twisted in what appeared to be obvious shock. He reached out and grabbed Gabriel's arm, his big thick fingers squeezing tightly. "Oh, my God, is she all right?"

Gabriel pulled his arm out of Thomas's grasp. "She's pretty banged up, but she's okay."

Thomas opened his door to allow them inside and out of the heat. "You can't believe that I had anything to do with that? I love Marlena." He gestured the two agents to an overstuffed sofa and fell into a chair as if his legs would no longer hold him. "She's really okay?"

"She'll be fine," Jackson said as he and Gabriel sat down.

"We understand you had an unpleasant conversation with her yesterday," Gabriel said, his gaze focused solely on Thomas's face and body language.

Thomas leaned back in the chair and shook his head. "It wasn't unpleasant, and it wasn't completely unexpected. I've never hidden my feelings for Marlena. I think she's a wonderful, beautiful woman. And I'd hoped that we could have a future together, but I also recognized that she wasn't at the same place I was, that she didn't love me like I love her. Yesterday she just confirmed to me what I already knew in my heart, that there was never going to be an *us* with me and Marlena."

"Did that make you angry?" Jackson asked.

"No, it made me very sad," Thomas replied without hesitation. He leaned forward, his features radiating with intense emotion. "I would never lift a finger to harm Marlena, whether she loved me or not. Even though she told me she'd never love me in a romantic way, I still love her and would never want to hurt her in any way."

"Where did you go yesterday after you left the bed-and-breakfast?" Gabriel asked.

"I went to the café and had a late lunch. You can check—I talked to half a dozen people while I was there, and I left the café with Chuck Gomez, who wanted an estimate for building a deck. I was at his place until after five."

"And if we check with Chuck, he'll tell us the same thing?" Jackson said.

"Of course he will, because it's the truth."

Gabriel believed him. As much as he wanted to, he didn't think that Thomas was responsible for Marlena's heart-stopping ride down the staircase.

Jackson rose from the sofa, as if knowing they were done here. The next step would be checking out the alibi Thomas had given them.

"I don't suppose it would be a good idea for me to see her," Thomas said as the two agents headed for the front door.

"No, I don't think that's a good idea," Gabriel replied. He wasn't sure if he didn't want Thomas around Marlena because he thought Thomas might be guilty of something or because he knew Thomas loved Marlena. He was surprised to find a tiny knot of jealousy residing deep inside his heart, one that flared bigger at the thought of Thomas and Marlena together.

"Any ideas?" he asked Jackson when they were back in the car together.

"I don't know. Maybe we should check out Pamela Winters again. I know it sounds crazy, but both attempts on Marlena feel feminine, if you know what I mean."

"I know exactly what you mean," Gabriel agreed, although he hadn't consciously thought about it until now. "I do know that it's fairly obvious that whoever is trying to hurt her is also trying to make it look accidental." He started the car so he could run the air conditioner to cool off the interior.

"But what would Pamela hope to gain now? The family is missing, and Marlena has already made it clear that she intends to leave town in the very near future." Gabriel frowned. "It doesn't make sense."

"Sometimes things just don't make sense. We both know that Pamela hates Marlena. Maybe Pamela doesn't trust that Marlena will really leave. Maybe Pamela believes that if the family is found safe and sound, then Daniella will talk Marlena into staying on as manager."

As the air conditioner began to blow cool air from the vents, Gabriel backed out of Thomas Brady's driveway. "Maybe we should check out Pamela's alibi for yesterday after she cleaned the bed-and-breakfast."

The last thing Gabriel wanted was to leave any stone unturned. Both attacks on Marlena had been attempted murder. Whether the threat against her was connected to the family disappearance wasn't clear.

All he knew was that when he thought of the bruising on Marlena's body, how lucky she was to be alive, he wanted—no, needed—somebody to pay for her pain.

Chapter Ten

Marlena awakened from her drug-induced sleep just after two in the afternoon, surprised to see Andrew sitting on the chair near her bed.

"Where's Gabriel?" she asked.

"He and Jackson left a while ago to talk to Thomas. Hey, are you hungry? I could whip us up a little afternoon snack." He rose from the chair.

She swallowed a smile. She had a feeling Andrew had been just waiting for any excuse to have a snack. "Actually, I am a little bit hungry," she replied, surprised to discover it was true. Although her body still ached from her fall down the stairs, her appetite apparently hadn't been affected.

Andrew reappeared minutes later with a platter of several kinds of cheese, some sliced salami and a variety of fruit cut into bite-size pieces. "I'll be right back with iced tea." He set the platter on the nightstand and then left her room again.

A few moments later he'd pulled his chair up closer and they were munching from the platter. "Those pain pills really knock you out," he said, and then popped a square of apple into his mouth.

"I've always had a low tolerance for any kind of pain medication."

"Cory came by to see you, but I sent him away with the assurance that you were resting comfortably."

"I'm sure he'll stop by later this evening." She tried to keep her mind off Gabriel. She didn't want to think about how gentle he'd been with her, the deep worry that had cut lines into his face and the anger that had darkened his eyes as she'd told him about Thomas.

"He won't kill Thomas, will he?" she asked half-seriously.

Andrew grinned. "Only if he has to, although if he finds out Thomas is the person who tried to kill you, then all bets are off."

"I just can't imagine Thomas being responsible for any of this. But I can't imagine *anyone* who would be responsible for these kinds of horrible things."

"That's because you're a nice woman. Nice people are always the ones who are totally blindsided by evil." He reached for a piece of salami. "I've seen a lot of crazy in my career as an agent. Nothing really surprises me anymore."

As they continued to consume the platter of food, they talked about Andrew's soon-to-be fiancée, some of the past cases the three-man team had worked on, and Jackson and Gabriel.

"Jackson is the proverbial Southern gentleman with the soul of a riverboat gambler," Andrew said with a laugh. "He's charming, has a reputation as a bit of a ladies' man and is sharp as a pin. Gabriel is the dark angel of our team. He's solitary, a lone wolf and has a heart that's made of coal."

"Is that another warning of some sort?" she asked.

Andrew shrugged. "Jackson and I both can't help but notice that there seems to be an…energy…between the two of you. Gabriel seems more invested in this case than in others. I don't know—maybe we're seeing something that isn't there, but I just wouldn't want to see you get hurt."

"I appreciate the concern, but I know exactly who Gabriel is and what he's not capable of giving." Besides, it was too late for her not to be hurt by him.

She wasn't sure when exactly in the span of nearly two weeks she'd given him her heart, but she recognized now that he owned it. She was in love with him.

It was late in the day when Gabriel came into her room, looking as tired and defeated as she'd ever seen him. He sat in the chair that had been pulled up by her bed and released a deep sigh.

"I'm assuming because you're here you didn't kill Thomas," she said, trying to alleviate some of the darkness in his eyes.

She succeeded. A smile lifted one corner of his mouth as he shook his head. "Nah. I managed to get through the entire day without killing anyone."

"Then that's a good day, right?" She reached out and grabbed his hand, unable to stop her need to connect with him.

He appeared surprised, but then wrapped his fingers around hers. "I would have at least liked to get somebody under arrest. That would have been a great day."

He stared down at their entwined fingers. "You put

it all out there, don't you? Despite your childhood and what happened in Chicago, you just go for it."

"It? You mean human connection? Love?"

He gave a curt nod.

"You know the old saying, 'I'd rather love and lose than never love at all'? That's what I believe. I believe you might have to kiss a lot of frogs, but eventually you find the prince who will love you as you need to be loved, who you'll love with all your heart and soul."

He started to pull his hand from hers, but she held tight. "It's okay. I know you don't believe the same thing I do. Although we share similar experiences of being abandoned by the women who should have loved us more than anyone or anything else on earth, we came out on the other side with very different views of love and relationships."

"Did you take a psychology lesson while I was gone this afternoon?" he asked drily.

She laughed, and then winced as her ribs protested. "Actually, I've had very little to do today besides sleep and think. You just happened to be what I thought about."

This time he managed to pull his hand away. "You shouldn't do that. You shouldn't waste time thinking about me."

"You might be a big bad FBI agent, but you don't get to dictate who I think about," she replied. She wasn't sure why, but she was feeling reckless. Maybe it was because she'd felt the brush of death on her neck one too many times.

"You should be thinking about why somebody pushed you into the pond, why somebody shoved you down the stairs." His voice was more forceful than the situation warranted.

"I know, and I've tried. But I can't come up with a name for you to make it all easier." She released a small sigh. "I've lost three people I love, and twice now somebody has tried to kill me, and I have no clue what's going on or who is responsible for any of it."

At that moment Cory appeared in the doorway, holding two tall glasses of chocolate milk. "Uh…want me to come back later?" he asked hesitantly.

"No, it's okay. I'm done here for now." Gabriel jumped up out of the chair as if he couldn't escape her fast enough. "I'll be in to check on you later," he said, and then with a nod to Cory he left the room.

"Chocolate milk always makes you feel better," Cory said as he sat in the chair Gabriel had vacated. He set one of the glasses on the nightstand and took a sip from his glass, then eyed her critically. "Do you feel as bad as you look?"

She smiled as she reached for the treat he'd prepared for them. "I'm stiff and sore, but at least I'm alive."

"Who is doing this, Marlena? Who and why?" Cory's eyes darkened. "I can't believe this has all happened to you."

"I wish somebody had some answers for me." She took a sip of her chocolate milk. "Mmm, you got it just right."

Cory grinned. "Yeah, one part milk and thirty parts chocolate. I know how you like it."

Marlena took another sip and then set the glass back on the nightstand. "I think tomorrow I'm going to talk to Gabriel and see if you and I are allowed to leave here. Who knows when or if Daniella, Sam and Macy will come back, and we can't just live in limbo until we have answers to what happened to them."

Cory frowned. "I'm going to miss hanging out with John when we leave."

"I know, but you'll make new friends. Besides, there's no reason why you couldn't drive back here on weekends occasionally to visit him."

Cory nodded and downed the last of his milk in several gulps. "Have you decided where we're heading?"

"Probably New Orleans." Her first choice had been Baton Rouge but she had changed her mind, knowing that's where Gabriel lived. She didn't want to run into him at a grocery store or see him on the streets. When she left here, she had to put him firmly out of her life forever.

"So when are we heading out?"

"Maybe by the end of next week."

"That soon?" Cory looked dismayed.

Marlena nodded her head. "It's time, Cory. We never planned to stay here forever, and it's time for us to move on. You need to get into a trade school, and I need to get started in some college classes. We can't do either of those things staying here."

"I know." He gestured toward her glass. "Finish your milk, and I'll take the glasses back into the kitchen."

She dutifully did as he asked. "We're going to be fine, Cory," she said as she handed him the empty glass.

He smiled at her. "We're the two musketeers, right? We've always been fine." He leaned down and pecked her on the forehead. "I'll check in on you in the morning. You rest like the doctor told you to."

"Don't worry. I have no desire to jump out of bed and do anything," she replied.

It was long after dinner when Marlena turned on her side and faced the window, where she could see the night shadows begin to take over the day.

Andrew had brought her a dinner tray earlier, but she'd only picked at the food. The chocolate milk that Cory had brought her earlier in the afternoon had filled her up.

It was time to take two more of the pain meds she'd been prescribed, but she wasn't ready to sleep yet and knew the pills would knock her out fairly quickly.

The truth of the matter was she had hoped Gabriel would stop in to tell her good-night, but as the darkness outside the window grew deeper and it got later and later, she realized he didn't intend to see her.

And why would he? she mentally scoffed. He didn't owe her a good-night or a sickroom visit or anything else. He was working his job, not babysitting her.

She sat up and shook out two of the pills, and then washed them down with a sip of water from a glass on her nightstand.

As she waited for the pills to take effect, her mind flew in a thousand directions. She knew initially it would be hard to leave here and start all over again, but it was what she'd always planned for, and now it was time to set those plans into motion.

Gabriel really was just a dream, not a man who had any place in her life. She'd be foolish to expect him to be anything else to her. He was an FBI agent sent here to solve a crime, not a man looking for a love interest.

Finally, her mind drifted back to those moments when she'd been in the pond, terrified that she would meet her death there, unable to save herself if Gabriel hadn't rushed to her rescue. Now she knew it had been an intentional shove, that somebody had wanted her to drown in the pond. She couldn't write it off as some sort of weird accident. It had definitely been attempted murder.

Drowsy now, she thought of that single second when she'd felt the hands on her back, hands that had shoved her at the top of the stairs. Who had done such a terrible thing? Who had wanted her dead?

Despite the sleepiness now nearly overwhelming her, a sliver of fear raced up her spine. Would there be another attempt? Was it possible that the third time would be a charm?

GABRIEL PACED THE length of the great room. Jackson was sprawled on the sofa watching television and Andrew was in the kitchen looking for a snack.

Gabriel had consciously chosen not to go in and tell Marlena good-night…because he'd wanted to, because he'd wanted her face to be the last thing he saw before he went to bed.

He felt like she was messing with his head, talking to him about love and such nonsense. For the first time since he'd been a young boy he felt vulnerable, and he didn't like it. He didn't like it at all.

He'd checked in with his director again late today and had the unpleasant duty of reporting that there was nothing to report in the disappearance of the former FBI agent and his family.

He had been instructed to remain in Bachelor Moon with his team until further notice. So here Gabriel was with no leads, nothing to do and nothing to think about except the woman who haunted him far too frequently.

At ten o'clock, both Jackson and Andrew headed upstairs to bed, and Gabriel sat at the dining room table with all the reports and copies of interviews they had generated while in Bachelor Moon.

Somehow, some way, they had to be missing something, an important piece of the puzzle that had been overlooked or thrown out as insignificant.

He was not only checking what they had in relation to the family disappearance but also to the attacks on Marlena, even though in his gut he didn't believe the two were connected.

He leaned back in the chair and blew a sigh of frustration. They only had three persons of interest at this point, Thomas Brady, Ryan Sherman and Pamela Winters, and there was no way that Pamela had any motive to harm the family—but she did have a motive to harm Marlena.

Marlena. He looked toward the kitchen and then checked his watch. It was almost eleven o'clock. She'd be asleep now. Maybe it was a good idea for him just to peek his head into her room and make sure she was okay.

Almost without conscious will, he rose to his feet and padded through the kitchen and to the door to her quarters. He told himself it was just his job to check on her, that it had nothing to do with any desire to see her, to watch her while she slept.

Whatever the reason, he knew he wouldn't sleep himself until he'd checked on her. Softly opening her door, he saw the small glow of the night-light in her room that led him unerringly to the side of her bed.

The faint light just reached her face, bathing her sleeping features in pale illumination. Who could ever want to hurt such a good, beautiful woman? Why would anyone want to douse her flame of life, of gentleness and caring?

He crept back out of the room, satisfied that he'd done his job. He'd seen that she was safe. He returned to the dining room, closed his laptop and shut the manila file of his materials on the table, then headed upstairs to bed.

Even as he slid beneath the lavender sheets, his mind whirled with elements of the crimes. What were they missing? Who had they overlooked? The only place they hadn't searched was John's little cottage because they'd had no legal reason to enter his home.

Was it possible the gardener was hiding something there? First thing in the morning, Gabriel intended to check it out. If John had nothing to hide, then he should allow the men inside to look around.

The other thing Gabriel had realized was that a little over two years ago, Daniella had been in the middle of a crime they knew little about other than what the sheriff and Marlena had told them. He needed to get the files from that particular crime and see if there were any clues in there that might yield some answers. He knew that Frank Mathis had been arrested for the murder of one woman and the kidnapping of Daniella and Macy, but was it possible Frank had had a partner?

That was his last thought before he fell asleep.

THE NEXT MORNING Gabriel, Jackson and Andrew stood on John's doorstep at seven-thirty. Gabriel knew that by eight the young man was usually someplace out on the property working, and he'd wanted to catch him before he left.

John opened the door, obviously surprised to see the three agents. "Hey, what's up?" he asked.

"You mind if we come in?" Gabriel asked.

"Sure." John opened the door to allow them inside the small cottage.

Gabriel's first impression was one of surprise at the tidiness of the living room. Although the sofa and recliner were worn and the wooden end tables had seen better days, there was nothing out of place, and the air smelled faintly of orange furniture polish.

"What's going on?" John asked as he gestured for them to sit. His eyes widened slightly. "Has something else happened to Marlena?"

"No, she's fine," Gabriel replied. None of them had taken John up on the offer of sitting. "Look, I'll be straight with you, John. This is one of the places we haven't checked to see if you have the Connellys shoved in a closet or locked in a room. So do you mind if we look around?"

John eyed him somberly. "I'd never do anything to hurt Sam and his family. There's not much to see, but you're welcome to search." He sank down on the sofa as the three men moved through the rest of the two-bedroom cottage.

The smallest room was obviously a guest room, with a single bed and a dresser and no closet space. The bathroom had a stand-up shower, no tub and a sink and stool.

It was easy to tell which room John used. Not only did it contain a double bed, but on the nightstand was a horticulture book, and a small bookshelf held more books about flowers, bushes and landscaping.

The three men returned to the living room to find John still seated on the sofa. "I didn't expect to find anything here, but I had to check," Gabriel said.

"I get it," John replied. "No stone unturned and all that. Don't worry, I'm not offended." He stood. "Is there anything else?"

"No, we're finished here," Gabriel said.

"Then I'll head out with you. Most days I have to haul Cory out of bed to get him on the grounds." John smiled and shook his head. "Kids."

"You know he's smoking pot," Gabriel said as they all started up the trail that led to the walkway around the pond.

"I know he dabbles a bit," John admitted. "I've been giving him hell about it. I think he's found some guys in town who party."

"Maybe it's a good thing Marlena is planning a move," Jackson said.

John shrugged. "If he wants to party, he'll find the party people wherever they move. But Cory has a good head on his shoulders. I think, once he gets into school, he'll buckle down to real life."

"For Marlena's sake, I hope you're right," Andrew said. "She definitely loves her brother."

They came to the place where they parted ways, John heading to Cory's small apartment around the back of the carriage house and Jackson, Andrew and Gabriel heading toward the car. It was going to be another long day of seeking clues to two crimes that had occurred at the cursed Bachelor Moon Bed-and-Breakfast.

Chapter Eleven

It had been two weeks and two days since the Connellys had gone missing, and five days since Marlena had been pushed down the stairs. The agents had spent the past couple of days doing what they'd been doing since their arrival—beating the bushes, walking the streets and coming up with nothing.

Gabriel had managed to keep his distance from Marlena, stepping into her room only when they arrived home after another disappointing day to keep her up-to-date. Her bruises had begun to change from the original violent purple to an ugly yellow, and he knew she was spending more time out of bed while they were gone during the daytime.

As usual, when he pulled into the parking lot just after six, a pall of frustration covered the three men in the car like a heavy old coat. Even Andrew's easy smile had been usurped by a weariness of expression they all felt.

They were men used to action, to finding answers to the most difficult questions, and yet they'd spent the past two weeks spinning in place like hamsters on wheels going nowhere.

Gabriel was surprised when they walked through

the front door and the scent of cooking filled the air. Since Marlena's crash down the stairs, dinner duty had fallen on Andrew's shoulders, but apparently Marlena was up and at work.

As the door closed behind them, she appeared in the dining room doorway. Gabriel tried not to notice how his heart gave a little jump at the sight of her.

"Should you be out of bed?" Jackson asked with concern.

She smiled. "If I spend another minute in that bed, you're all going to have to lock me in a padded room because I'll go out of my mind."

Gabriel didn't want to be captured by the warmth of her smile. He didn't want to feel a rush of heat as his gaze lingered first on her face and then swept the length of her.

She wore a white-and-green-striped T-shirt that hid the last of the bruises on her torso, along with jeans, which hid those that had marred her hips and thighs.

"I've got hamburgers just about ready, so dinner can be served within the next ten minutes or so," she said.

"Sounds good," Andrew said. Together he and Jackson headed upstairs while Gabriel followed her as she turned and went back into the kitchen.

"Are you sure you feel well enough to be out of bed?" he asked as she removed a large pot of baked beans from the oven and set it on the stovetop.

"I'm still a little stiff and sore, but it's past time for me to be up and around." She didn't look at him as she removed the hamburger patties from the skillet and set them on a plate already filled with burgers. "I think I needed to get up and work out the last of the kinks."

She sidestepped him to open the refrigerator and pull out ketchup and mustard bottles, then set them on the counter. "I'm assuming there's nothing new to report."

She finally looked at him, her green eyes pleasant yet distant.

"Nothing." He held out a thick file folder that he'd carried in with him. "I finally decided to go back to when Daniella was kidnapped and look at everything Sheriff Thompson had on file about that crime."

"Surely you can't think what's happening now is tied to that. The man responsible for Daniella and Macy's kidnapping is behind bars."

"I know." He heard the frustration in his own voice. "We've gone over everything with a fine-tooth comb. We've interviewed and reinterviewed most all the people in Bachelor Moon and we've come up empty-handed." He dropped the fat file on the nearby table. "This is my last gasp, my reaching for straws in an effort to gain some answers."

"I hope you find something." She pulled a platter of sliced tomatoes from the refrigerator and then faced him again. "I've been meaning to ask you when Cory and I can leave here. We can't just wait around forever for something to happen. We have to get on with our lives."

"You're still part of an ongoing crime," he replied. He hated the distance he felt emanating from her even as he recognized he'd been the one who'd put it there.

She tilted her head slightly, her eyes confused. "So what does that mean? Can we leave or not? I would think if somebody is trying to kill me here, then probably the best thing I could do is leave."

"But what if the person follows you? Then you'll be vulnerable." Gabriel had no idea if he spoke from his head or his heart; he only knew he didn't want her alone in some big city without closure as to what was happening here in Bachelor Moon.

"Then is that a no? We can't leave yet?"

"Give us one more week," he finally relented, and knew it was more than a professional request. He didn't want to see her go. He didn't want to be here without seeing her smiling face, basking in the warmth of spirit that wafted from her.

"One week," she agreed. "Now you better go get washed up while I get the food on the table."

He left the kitchen with a sense of something lost, something that might have been precious if he'd allowed it. But he couldn't allow it. It would be foolhardy for him to pretend that he could be the man for her, that he was capable of giving her what she wanted, what she desperately needed in her life.

He didn't want her to go, and yet he needed to get her away from him. As he washed up and headed back down the stairs, he was determined to continue maintaining the almost painful distance he'd created between them.

Dinner was a silent affair. The three agents had run out of things to say to each other and so they ate without conversation. Gabriel was about halfway through the meal when he realized Marlena was humming in the kitchen. It was an old standard song about love, and her pitch was perfect.

The sound wrapped a chord of desire around Gabriel's heart and stole away the last of his appetite. He could imagine himself next to her in bed after they'd made love, her soft humming lulling him to sleep. The pleasure of the vision pulled a visceral response from him, one that he'd never felt before.

With a murmured excuse, he left the table and went upstairs to his room, needing to be alone, the way he had always been.

He sat on the bed, cursing the fact that he'd left the file on Daniella and Macy's kidnapping on the kitchen table. He could have holed up here for the rest of the night if he had the file.

Instead he stretched out on the bed and stared up at the ceiling, his thoughts so scattered he couldn't focus on any one thing.

Somehow during the past two weeks, he'd realized at his very core he was a lonely man, afraid to reach out to others, having grown comfortable in his isolation. It didn't feel as comfortable as it used to.

Marlena had banged against the armor of his heart over and over again, denting it to unrecognizable properties. He couldn't let her pierce through the steel that had been forged so many years before.

He didn't know how long he'd been on the bed when a soft knock fell on his door and Jackson peeked his head in. "You okay?"

Gabriel sat up on the bed. "Sure, I'm fine. Why?"

"You scooted out of the dining room pretty fast." Jackson eased down in the chair next to the bed. "She's gotten to you, hasn't she?"

Gabriel didn't even try to pretend to play stupid.

"Maybe a little," he admitted. "But it's not going anywhere."

"Why not? It's obvious she's into you and you're into her. Why not take a chance, Gabriel? Aren't you tired of being alone at the end of each day?"

Gabriel raised an eyebrow. "I could say the same thing about you. You're a good-looking guy. Why aren't you married?"

"Thanks for noticing that I am rather hot," Jackson replied with an easy, facetious grin. The grin lingered only a moment and then fell away. "The problem with you is that you don't love. The problem with me is that I love all women. I haven't found the single woman I want to share my bed with every night and wake up with every morning yet. But I know eventually I will. I think you've already found yours, but you refuse to acknowledge it even to yourself."

"Jackson, I appreciate your concern for my personal life, but I figure within a couple of weeks, we'll be out of here. Marlena had her own life planned and I'll go back to mine. It's best that way. She deserves more than I could ever give her."

"You sell yourself too short, Gabriel," Jackson said as he rose from the chair.

"I'm fine with my life, but I do appreciate your concern." Gabriel got up from the bed.

Jackson cast him his legendary lazy smile. "Hey, that's what partners are for. Are you coming back downstairs?"

"Actually, I think I'll take a little walk before it gets dark. Maybe some fresh air will help clear my head."

He followed Jackson down the stairs and as he sat down on the sofa, Gabriel walked out the front door.

The air certainly wasn't fresh but rather the usual hot and humid blanket that had been unrelenting for the past two weeks. At least out here he couldn't hear the sound of her melodic humming as she cleaned up the kitchen, and he couldn't smell the scent of her that made an aching need throb inside his veins.

He didn't want to take a chance with her. He didn't want to be another man who let her down, another man who broke her heart. He cared about her enough not to be that man.

He waved to Cory and John, who appeared to be storing their shears, hoes and landscaping equipment in the shed. Sam and Daniella must have been special people, because everyone who worked for them continued to keep the place in pristine order.

Gabriel didn't believe they were coming back. In his heart, in the depth of his soul, he'd already realized they had to be dead.

What happened to the bed-and-breakfast after he and his team left wasn't his problem. Eventually it would be in the hands of lawyers and probate courts to decide what to do with the business and with the property.

Marlena and Cory would also be long gone by then, living a new life in a new city. He was certain that she would meet the man she'd dreamed about, a man who would not only be her best friend but also her lover, her husband. He wanted that for her, and yet he couldn't halt the pain that pierced his heart.

He paused at the end of the walkway and stared into

the murky, dark pond water, the sun at an angle where he couldn't see his own reflection.

He wasn't sure how long he stood there lost in thoughts when he gazed again at the water, this time not only seeing his own reflection but that of Marlena standing just behind him. He jumped in surprise and turned to face her.

"I'm sorry. I didn't mean to startle you," she said. She held out a tall glass of lemonade. "I just thought you might find this refreshing."

He frowned even as he took the drink from her. "You've got to stop doing things like this." He started up the walkway toward the porch, aware of her following close behind him.

"Doing things like what?" she asked, looking genuinely puzzled.

He didn't reply until he sat in one of the chairs on the porch and set the drink on the table beside him. She sat next to him.

"Doing things like what?" she repeated.

"Nice things. Thoughtful things. And I wish you wouldn't hum when you worked in the kitchen."

She stared at him as if he'd lost his mind, and perhaps he had. "My humming bothers you?"

"Yeah, it does. It sounds nice, but it's irritating." He knew he was being a jerk, and yet he couldn't help it.

"Does my sitting out here next to you bother you?" she asked, her eyes narrowed slightly as if in thought.

He looked out at the pond again, unable to watch her features when he replied. "Yeah, actually, it does."

"Then I'll just head back inside." She jumped out

of the chair and disappeared into the house before he could form the words to stop her.

He turned and stared at the glass of lemonade she'd brought him. Damn her for making him want her, and damn him for wanting her. He didn't just want to taste her lips again, feel her naked body moving against his own. He wanted her thoughts, her dreams. He wanted to be her best friend and her lover. More than anything, he wanted to be strong enough to reach out for love, but the truth was that when it came to matters of the heart, he was nothing but a coward.

MARLENA STOMPED BACK inside and sank down at the kitchen table, her feelings stinging from his words. Her humming bothered him? Tomorrow night when she fixed dinner, she'd sing at the top of her lungs, and the next time she made him a glass of lemonade, she'd pour it over his handsome head.

She finally decided to take her hurt feelings and go to her own rooms. She would watch a little television and then get a long night of rest. Although her bruises were starting to fade, she still felt as if she'd been run over by a truck. She'd stopped taking the pain pills during the day, but took a couple at night to help her sleep.

Maybe tonight the pills would not only ease the ache of her muscles but also banish the pain in her heart. Loving Gabriel wasn't hard. Realizing he didn't have the capacity to love her back was devastating.

She settled onto the sofa in her private sitting room and tuned the television to one of the few sitcoms she thought was funny. But tonight no laughter escaped her lips. In fact, she found herself drifting off in thought rather than watching television.

One week.

She only had to see his handsome face, to smell his familiar scent and to be around him for one more week, and then she and Cory would be free to leave here.

The sadness that she would pack in her suitcase would make a heavy load if it had true weight. She would carry with her the ache of absence for the loss of Sam and Daniella and Macy. And she would take with her a heart filled with love for a man incapable of loving her back.

Her love for Gabriel had been formed by a hundred different elements. While their lust for each other had certainly been undeniable, over the past two weeks she'd also fallen in love with his dry sense of humor and the soft vulnerability he certainly didn't realize occasionally shone from his eyes.

It was impossible to dissect why she loved Gabriel. She just did. It was as simple and as complicated as that. She was about to go to bed when she heard a soft knock at her door.

"Come in," she said.

Gabriel stepped into her room. "Mind if I have a seat if I plan on offering up an apology?"

She wanted to be angry with him, but he truly looked contrite, and she just couldn't summon any emotion except the love that threatened to bubble out of her.

"Sounds like a fair trade," she replied and made room for him on the sofa.

He sank down as if he weighed a thousand pounds. "I'm sorry. I acted like a jerk earlier."

"Yes, you did," she agreed easily. "You're lucky I'm not a woman who holds a grudge. And tomorrow morning when I make your breakfast, I promise you I'm not going to hum. I'm going to sing at the top of my lungs just because it will aggravate you."

"Your humming doesn't aggravate me. This case has aggravated me, and you were a handy scapegoat." He raked a hand through his thick hair and leaned back. "As if Sam's family's disappearance isn't enough, we still haven't figured out why anyone would want to hurt you."

"Maybe because they heard me humming?" she said in an effort to bring a smile to his face.

It worked. His sensual lips curved upward and he released a small laugh. "You aren't going to let me off the hook, are you?"

"You're off the hook. I just wanted to see your smile." Her love for him pressed hard against her chest and teased on the tip of her tongue with the need to be released, with the intense desire to be spoken aloud. "I care about you, Gabriel."

His smile fell away, and instead a deep frown cut across his forehead.

"It upsets you that I care about you."

"That's your problem, not mine," he scoffed.

"I know, but you can't do anything about how I feel about you. You can't stop me from caring about you, from wanting to comfort you when you're sad, from sharing your laughter when you're happy. You can't stop me from falling in love with you, Gabriel, and I am in love with you."

His shoulders stiffened defensively. "Those pain pills you've been taking have definitely addled your mind." It was obvious he was uncomfortable with the conversation. He twisted on the sofa as if to gain more distance from her, as if afraid she might decide to reach out and touch him in some way.

"It's okay, Gabriel. You don't have to do anything about it. You don't even have to care. I just want you to know that you are loved, that you're worth something and that somebody cares about you and wants you to find happiness."

For the first time since she'd met him, he appeared speechless and more than a little bit stunned. "Why are you telling me this?" he finally asked.

"I don't know. I just felt like I needed you to know. Maybe it's because I've been reminded in the past weeks how fragile life is and I wanted you to know how I felt about you if something happens and I don't get a chance to tell you. Consider it a gift from me to you."

"Nothing is going to happen to you," he said firmly.

"I hope not, but there are no guarantees, and you have to admit you don't have a clue who might have tried to hurt me."

"After talking to Thomas, we went by Pamela Winter's place to speak with her." It was an obvious attempt for him to guide the conversation away from personal things and back to the reason he was here at the bed-and-breakfast. "Her alibi for the time that you were pushed down the stairs is that she was at home alone.

She received no phone calls, nobody saw her, so there's no way for us to know if she's telling the truth or not."

"I don't understand. What would Pamela hope to gain by killing me now? Daniella is gone, and in one week, Cory and I are heading out of here."

Gabriel shrugged. "We figured maybe Pamela doesn't believe you're really going to leave."

"I don't know. Considering that Daniella is missing, it just doesn't make sense to me that Pamela would do something like this."

"I can't figure any of this out, but I know you're wrong about me." He stood. "My own mother decided I wasn't worth loving, and nobody has made me feel any different about myself since then."

Her heart ached as she heard the empty hollowness in his voice. "I could," she said softly. "I do."

"Hey, sis." Cory's voice came from nearby. He appeared in the doorway holding two glasses of chocolate milk. He stopped short as he saw Gabriel. "Oh, is this a bad time?"

"No, I was just leaving." Gabriel shot out of the room as if he'd just been looking for a reason to make a hasty retreat.

As he left, he took her heart. She'd laid it all out on the line, had spoken the words of love that had burned inside her, and he'd refused to either accept or return that love to her.

What shocked her was that she'd believed she was prepared for exactly the response she'd gotten from him. She hadn't been prepared for the sweeping heartache that filled her as she watched him leave.

Chapter Twelve

She loved him.

Gabriel had left her sitting area and had immediately gone upstairs to his own room, where he'd paced the small confines and tried to erase her words of love from his mind.

Somehow her actually saying it out loud had shocked him, but if he looked deep in his heart, he'd already known she was falling in love with him. He'd seen it in her eyes when she gazed at him, had felt it in the most simple of touches.

He'd warned her in a dozen ways not to love him, that he was incapable of returning that emotion, but it obviously hadn't made any difference to her.

One week, he told himself. In a week she'd be gone. She and Cory would leave here the way they had arrived: in her beat-up old car, with a suitcase full of clothes. The only difference was she'd leave with enough money to start a new life.

She would not leave with him, and he refused to return her gift of love back to her. It was her problem, not his, and she would just have to fall out of love with him.

Once he felt as if he had his wayward emotions under control, he went back downstairs to retrieve the information about Daniella and Macy's kidnapping. He knew it was a long shot that he'd find anything in that paperwork to help with the current situation, but he had to do something, and at least it might take his mind off Marlena.

It was just after nine when he took off his gun and holster and sat at the dining room table with the folder in front of him. Marlena's door was closed, indicating that Cory had left and she was probably in bed.

Andrew had gone upstairs a few minutes earlier, and Jackson was planted on the sofa in the common room watching the end of an old movie.

Other than the distant sound of the television drifting through the air, the house was silent. For several long moments he sat with his eyes closed, playing and replaying every second he'd spent with Marlena.

For the first time in his life he'd felt softness, he'd experienced kindness and, yes, he'd felt the nudge of love attempting to take possession of his heart.

With an irritated sigh, he opened his eyes and stared at the thick folder on the table in front of him. *First things first,* he thought, deciding to make a small pot of coffee before delving into the elements of a case that had occurred over two years before.

The coffee was dripping into the carafe when Jackson stepped into the kitchen. "I'm heading off to bed, unless you want me to help you go through that material."

"Nah. I'll be fine by myself." Gabriel stepped closer to the coffeepot that had finished making the four cups that should see him through the rest of the night. "I'll catch you in the morning."

Jackson nodded. "Good night, Gabriel."

Gabriel poured his coffee and returned to the dining room table. This time the silence of the house was complete around him. He took a sip of coffee and opened the file.

Within minutes he had disappeared into the crime that had occurred so long ago, a crime that had brought two people to love but not before danger had struck.

As Gabriel read, he scribbled away in his own notebook, noting the people who had been players in Daniella's drama and listing who of those players was still around.

He paused occasionally to sip his coffee and stare out the nearby window, fighting thoughts of Marlena and her words of love for him.

Was it truly possible that he could be loved, that he wasn't a throwaway child who had become a tossed-away man? Had he so embraced the fact that his mother hadn't wanted him, that his father had needed to beat him, that he'd never let go of that baggage? That he'd become what they'd indicated him to be? Not worth caring about, not worth loving? So then, why could Marlena believe herself in love with him?

At thirty-four years old, he was far too old to change his ways now. He was alone and had always been alone. Besides, Marlena was in a state of transition and grief. Her friends had been missing for over two weeks, and her own life had been threatened twice. With all that emotion inside her, she was probably grasping onto something solid, and he just happened to be there.

Feeling a little better, being able to rationalize away Marlena's words of love, he got another cup of coffee, and then left the dining room and headed to the bathroom just off the common area.

Once there he sluiced cool water over his face in an effort to fight the drowsiness that had begun to overtake him as he'd pored over the notes, lists of evidence and interviews.

He leaned back against the door, wondering how it was possible that three trained, professional FBI agents couldn't get a grasp on what had happened here.

They had worked many cases together and separately in the past, and they'd always closed the case, found the bad guy and seen him or her thrown in jail.

But this case had them all stymied, spinning around like Keystone Kops, hoping to bump into a bad guy. He splashed water on his face once again, dried off and then left the bathroom.

He walked back through the common room and returned to the dining room table, where he focused on the crime of Daniella and Macy's kidnapping.

Frank Mathis had obviously been psychotic. He'd not only killed Daniella's first husband, Johnny, but he'd believed Daniella and Macy were destined to be his own family.

He'd managed to get in through the window of the rooms Marlena now called home, then had dragged Daniella and Macy outside and carried them away.

As the investigation had continued, Frank hadn't even been on the list of suspects until Sam had run out of potentials and had begun to look at the gardener more closely.

Sam, along with Sheriff Thompson, had finally decided to follow Frank home, and on that night they'd discovered that what had been an old storm shelter in the ground near Frank's cottage had been transformed into a bunkerlike apartment where Daniella and Macy had been locked away.

Gabriel sat up straighter in the chair. A bunker? Hidden someplace near the cottage? He hadn't heard anything about it until now.

He doubted that John, the current gardener, even knew it was there. He stared out the window to the darkness beyond. Did Marlena know about the bunker? Had its existence simply slipped her mind?

Was it possible that the Connelly family could be that close? Held for some reason on their own property in a secret bunker under the ground?

Adrenaline shot through him as his gaze searched outside the window where the darkness was profound. How could he find a secret bunker at night when he didn't know precisely where it was?

And why hadn't Sheriff Thompson mentioned the place where Daniella and Macy had been confined? Did the man have one foot so far out the door into retirement that he'd missed an important element to share with the agents who had taken over the latest crime?

Again he glanced at Marlena's door. Was it possible she was still awake? That she might be able to pinpoint for him the entrance to the underground bunker?

There was only one way to find out. He knocked softly on the door that led into her private quarters, unsurprised when he didn't hear an answering response.

He grabbed hold of the knob and breathed a sigh of relief as it turned in his hand. He opened it and followed the faint glow of the night-light that shone from her bedroom.

It was just a little after eleven. Maybe she wasn't so deeply asleep that he could wake her enough to find out what she knew.

Surely Daniella would have talked about her time in captivity. She might have taken Marlena to the place near the cottage where Frank Mathis had held her and Macy against their wills.

Silently he crept toward her bedroom door. If he couldn't get the answers he needed from her now, then he'd get the good sheriff and some of his men out here with lights to find the cellar door apparently built into the earth.

He took a step into Marlena's room and instantly froze in horrified shock. Marlena was in the bed, but she wasn't alone. In the pale illumination from the night-light, he could see the slithering of snakes at all four corners of the bed. They were not just any snakes, but cottonmouths—poisonous, deadly snakes.

Two things instantly pierced through his shock. First, Marlena lay on her back, not moving. He couldn't even be sure if she was breathing. Second, his gun. He needed his gun.

As he took a step backward, the snakes coiled and vibrated their tails as their mouths gaped open to display a startling whiteness.

Afraid of moving too fast and agitating them further, with agonizing slowness he backed out of the room and then raced toward the dining room where he'd left his gun on the table.

She'd looked dead. Had the cottonmouth snakes already bitten her enough times to deliver sufficient venom to stop her heart? His hand shook as he grabbed his gun, and then he crept silently back to her bedroom doorway.

The snakes stirred with ominous intent. It was like a picture from a nightmare, the snakes guarding the innocent princess…or determined to keep her as their own.

The only sounds in the room were the snakes' hissing and the thunder of his heartbeat. His hand slickened with nervous sweat as he tightened his grip on the gun, trying to decide if he could shoot one without the other three striking at her, if he could kill one without the bullet winging her at the same time.

A fear he'd never known backed up in his throat, making him feel nauseous as he tried to make a decision, any decision that would do no more harm to Marlena than had already been done.

His aversion to snakes disappeared as his only thought was to get them away from her. She had yet to move, making him worry he was already too late.

He stared at the snake closest to where he stood. Could he grab it by the tail and pull it off the bed without stirring up the others? He had to do something. If Marlena had been bitten, then she needed emergency care as soon as possible.

Despite his own healthy fear and repugnance of snakes, he knew he couldn't stand by any longer. With a deep breath, he grabbed the tail of the nearest snake and whirled around to smash it against the nearby wall. He turned quickly and shot the snake at the top of the bed closest to Marlena.

As he popped off two more shots to kill the others, he was vaguely aware of the rumble of footsteps. The air smelled of cordite and snake guts, and one more lingering odor.

As Jackson raced into the room and flipped on the overhead light, he gasped in stunned surprise.

"What the hell?" Andrew said from behind him.

"Call the sheriff and call for an ambulance," Gabriel cried as he dropped his gun and then rushed to Marlena's side. The deafening gunshots hadn't awakened her. She hadn't moved during the entire drama, and that terrified him.

"Marlena." He touched her face and still she didn't stir, although he was grateful to realize that she was breathing—but that didn't mean she wasn't in grave danger.

He had no idea if the snakes had been beneath her covers, if there were bite marks he couldn't see, but he was also afraid to move her, afraid that doing so would make her heart pump faster, make the venom flow more freely through her veins.

"Sheriff Thompson and an ambulance are on the way," Andrew said from the doorway.

"Marlena, open your eyes." Gabriel fell to his knees at the side of the bed, his gaze focused solely on the woman there and how dead she already looked. "Marlena, for God's sake, wake up." Anguish squeezed his heart so hard he could scarcely breathe.

Jackson placed a hand on his shoulder. "Gabriel,

get up. She's not going to wake up." Gabriel shot him a frantic glance.

"She's not sleeping. She's unconscious."

Gabriel stumbled to his feet and fought against a burning pain in his eyes, the squeezing vise of his heart. How had this happened? She'd told him she loved him—she couldn't die now.

"I came in…and she was there on the bed, with four snakes next to her.… I shot three of them.…" His voice trailed off, and then he continued, "They didn't end up in here accidentally."

Within minutes the ambulance arrived, and two stocky paramedics moved Marlena from the bed to a stretcher. They were focused on their victim, professional in their demeanor. Neither of them mentioned the dead snake parts and guts that littered the room.

As they wheeled Marlena to the awaiting ambulance, Gabriel ran after them. At the same time, Sheriff Thompson arrived and got out of his car. Obviously the call had pulled him out of bed. His shirt was half-buttoned, and his thin gray hair stood on end. "What's going on?" he asked.

"Talk to Jackson and Andrew," Gabriel said as he started to climb into the back of the ambulance, only to be stopped by one of the paramedics.

"Nobody can ride back here. Regulations and all that," he said. He slammed the back door and the ambulance backed up to leave.

Gabriel fumbled in his pocket, grateful that he still had the car keys. Ignoring the sheriff, he raced for his car. He had to be with her. He had to see if she made it to the hospital alive.

GABRIEL SAT IN the hospital waiting room alone, after explaining to the doctor that it was possible Marlena had suffered numerous cottonmouth bites.

He'd been thankful that she'd still been breathing when they'd taken her back to the examining room. And as he waited to see that she would survive this night, new emotions warred inside him.

Seated in an uncomfortable yellow plastic chair, he recognized that he loved her, that he would always care about what happened to her. That didn't mean he intended to walk side by side with her for the rest of her life, but it did mean he was capable of loving and being loved, and that was an epiphany he'd have to explore another time.

The second emotion that built up inside him was rage of overwhelming proportions. Somebody had wanted those snakes to bite her, to deposit their venom inside her and kill her.

Somebody had wanted her dead, and he believed he now knew who that somebody was. The only reason he wasn't going after the person now was because he had to know if Marlena lived. He had to know if he was going to beat the hell out of somebody for a murder or an attempted-murder rap.

And he wanted to beat the hell out of somebody. He wanted to cause pain to the person who had been behind the attacks on Marlena. He needed to know why, and he needed to know if that person was also responsible for the Connellys' probable deaths, too.

If he was doing his job correctly, he would have called Jackson and Andrew to capture the culprit. He would have called Sheriff Thompson to make an arrest. But he didn't want this done correctly. Selfishly, it needed to be him who faced the perpetrator.

He jumped out of his chair as Dr. Sheldon approached him. "Is she going to be okay?" Gabriel asked before the doctor could say a word.

"We checked every inch of her body and couldn't find a single snake bite," he said.

The air blew out of his lungs with relief, but it lasted only a second as he stared at the doctor. "Then why isn't she awake?"

"She's definitely unconscious. I've taken some blood and we're running tests, but it's my belief that she's been drugged."

Gabriel's blood ran cold even though he'd suspected as much. Drugged and left alone in a bed with vipers—the only reason for that was a murder attempt. Those snakes hadn't crawled in through the back door.

"Needless to say, she'll be staying here for the night. We'll monitor her, and hopefully by tomorrow afternoon she'll have metabolized whatever she was given and will be awake." The doctor frowned, as if he wasn't sure she'd ever awaken.

"I'll be back later tonight or first thing in the morning," Gabriel said, not wanting to hear anything bad the doctor might have to say. He simply couldn't handle the idea of Marlena never waking up. "You make sure you take good care of her."

"We're going to take very good care of her," the doctor assured him.

With a curt nod, Gabriel turned on his heels and headed for the exit, his rage building. He couldn't wait to get back to the bed-and-breakfast. He was certain that he knew who was responsible for the attacks on Marlena. He just couldn't figure out why.

Before this night was over he'd have his answers, and before the sun rose, the culprit would be behind bars. Of that he was determined.

Chapter Thirteen

Gabriel walked into the bed-and-breakfast to find Jackson, Andrew and Sheriff Thompson sitting in the common room. All three men stood at his appearance. "Is she going to be all right?" Andrew asked worriedly.

"The doctor couldn't find any snake bites on her, so she should be fine, although he believes she was drugged." He looked at the sheriff. "I suggest you get some men out here and process that bedroom. It's definitely a crime scene."

He was vaguely irritated that he had to tell the man to do his job, that Thompson wouldn't already have called out men to begin his own investigation into Marlena's near-death experience.

"I didn't know if this was something you all wanted to handle or you wanted my men to handle," Thompson replied.

"We're here to investigate the disappearance of a family. These attacks on Marlena fall under your jurisdiction," Jackson replied.

Maybe legally, but there was no way Gabriel intended to allow the lazy, mostly retired sheriff to do what needed to be done for Marlena.

"John and Cory aren't here?" he said, stating the obvious.

"We figured they either haven't heard the commotion or are out somewhere together in town," Jackson replied.

Gabriel nodded and then turned his attention back to Sheriff Thompson. "The first thing you might want to collect is the glass on her nightstand. If she was drugged, I imagine you'll find trace evidence of it in that glass," Gabriel said. "And I've got to get my gun. I dropped it after I killed those snakes."

He didn't wait for a reply but went back into Marlena's bedroom. The sight of the dead snakes fed the rage that filled him. He grabbed his gun from the floor near the bed and then walked into the kitchen to grab a flashlight he'd seen beneath the sink. Armed, he went into the dining room table to pull on his holster.

He was about to go hunting.

As he stepped back into the common room, Jackson looked pointedly at his gun in the holster. "What have you got in mind?"

"I want you and Andrew to oversee the evidence gathering in the bedroom. I'm going for a walk."

Jackson's eyes narrowed. "You need your gun to go for a walk?"

Gabriel shot him a cold, bloodless smile. "You never know when you might need to shoot a snake." He slid out the door and into the darkness of the night.

Thankfully the moon was a bright half sphere, spilling down enough illumination that he didn't need to use the flashlight. The first place he went was to Cory's small apartment, although he knew if the young man had been there, he would have heard the gunshots and come running.

He knocked three times before confirming that Cory wasn't inside, which meant he was probably down at the cottage with John, the great snake hunter.

As he walked the pathway around the pond, Gabriel knew he'd gone rogue, that he should have his partners out here by his side. But this was personal, and he wanted to finish it for Marlena's sake, for his own sake.

As he walked past the area of the pond where he'd dragged Marlena to the shore, he balled his hands into fists. As he thought of her lying on the floor at the foot of the stairs after having been pushed, he wanted to slam his fists into somebody's face.

He knew he had to push past the rage and instead reach for the cold professionalism that had always gotten him through difficult cases.

No emotion, just get the job done. No thoughts of Marlena, or Sam and Daniella and little Macy, just get the job done. It was a mantra that calmed him as he reached the end of the walkway where the path veered into the woods that would eventually lead to John's cottage.

Here he needed his flashlight, and he cupped the beam with his hand to allow him to maneuver with a minimal amount of light. What if Marlena wasn't just unconscious, but rather was in some kind of overdose coma? His heart beat the rhythm of an agony he'd never known before.

He shoved these thoughts away, needing to focus on the here and now and nothing else. He'd just reached the bottom of the path. John's cottage was on his left, and he took several steps toward it but then paused as he saw a flash of light just to his right.

He turned off his flashlight, and in the moonlight that filtered down through the trees, he saw two figures magically appear as if spewed out of the earth.

The bunker. His heart pounded so loud he was surprised John and Cory couldn't hear it. They were laughing about something, but their laughter halted as Gabriel stepped into the moonlight, his gun in hand.

"What's going on, boys?" The question shot out of him like a bullet.

The two froze, and then suddenly John took off in the direction of the cottage and Cory ran up the walkway that Gabriel had just come down.

With a muttered curse, Gabriel holstered his gun and took off after Marlena's brother. He wasn't about to shoot him in the back, but he definitely wanted to get him into custody.

Cory was fast, but Gabriel was driven by the sheer adrenaline of a desire for justice, the need for answers. He chased Cory around the pond and finally managed to tackle him in the lawn at the side of the parking lot.

"Leave me alone," Cory cried as he managed to escape Gabriel's hold. They both got to their feet as Jackson, Andrew and Sheriff Thompson came out on the porch.

"Why did you do it, Cory? Why are you trying to kill your sister?"

Cory looked around wildly and then back at Gabriel. "I don't know what you're talking about."

"I smelled you, Cory. I can smell you now, and it's the same odor I noticed when I first walked into your sister's room and saw those snakes on her bed. It was the scent of pot lingering in the air."

"You're crazy," Cory replied, his boyish features twisted in anger in the moonlight.

"No, but I think you might be crazy for trying to kill your own sister, for trying to hurt a woman who has nothing but kindness and love in her heart."

Cory's eyes narrowed, and his features became almost feral. "She doesn't love me. She's just had to put up with me. Eventually she'll leave me like my mother did. She'll find a man or get a good job. She wants to drag me to some other town and make me get on with my life so she doesn't have to take care of me anymore."

It was as if a dam had broken. "I hate her. I wish she was dead. I don't love her. All she's ever done is make my mom go away and nag me all the time. I'll never love anyone except myself, and she was screwing up what I wanted for my own life. Well, screw her."

"I'd say you've managed to screw up your own life," Gabriel replied. He took a step closer to Cory. "Thompson, toss me your handcuffs."

The cuffs landed in the grass near Gabriel, and as he bent to pick them up, Cory stepped forward and delivered an uppercut to Gabriel's jaw that nearly threw him to his back.

Gabriel had been containing himself, trying to go easy on Cory for Marlena's sake, but with that single punch to his jaw, Cory had changed all the rules.

Gabriel grabbed the cuffs and then tackled Cory once again. He planted his fist in Cory's nose, hearing a satisfying crunch. As Cory screamed, Gabriel flipped him over on his belly and cuffed him behind his back.

Gabriel pulled him up off the ground.

"You broke my nose," Cory cried.

"You want to be a big tough murderer, suck it up, big guy," Gabriel returned. He looked up at the porch, where none of the three men had moved from their positions.

"Thompson, come and get this trash and take him to your jail. I'll be in touch with you later." He motioned for Jackson and Andrew to follow him, and then Gabriel turned and hurried back around the pond.

"Where are we going?" Andrew asked.

"To a secret underground bunker where I hope we'll find the Connelly family alive." Gabriel's jaw ached, and his heart hurt for Marlena. If and when she awakened, she'd discover that it had been her own brother who had tried to kill her.

"An underground bunker?"

"Yeah. While I was reading through the old file on Daniella and Macy's kidnapping, I found out they were kept in an underground bunker someplace here. I came to check it out and just happened to see Cory and John coming up from it."

"Where's John now?" Jackson asked as they started down the path toward the cottage.

"He ran the opposite way of Cory, and my first goal was to get Cory under arrest. I don't know what part John played in what's happened, but he shouldn't be too hard to find even if he runs all the way to a different state," Gabriel replied.

They veered off to the narrow trail that led to the

cottage, and when they reached the end of it, the bunker door was still open, emitting a faint glow of light.

"Wow," Andrew exclaimed. "Who would have thought?"

Gabriel's heart began a new bang of anxiety...and of hope. "I just want to find the family safe and secure, and this definitely seems like a likely place to keep them."

"Let's just hope they're all okay," Jackson said softly.

The door led to a set of earthen stairs that went down to another door. The one at the bottom was secured with a padlock. "Stay here," Gabriel told the other men as he drew his gun.

He went down the stairs and placed his ear against the wooden door, praying that he might hear one of the Connelly family members crying out for help, anything that would indicate there were people alive on the other side of the door.

He heard nothing. He moved to one side of the small tunnel and aimed his gun at the padlock, hoping to hell that the bullet didn't ricochet back to kill him.

He shot off the lock, grateful to find himself still standing after the flash and bang that nearly deafened him. The lock hung in pieces, and as he waited for them to cool off, Jackson and Andrew moved to stand just behind him.

"I hope we open this door to find Sam and Daniella and Macy being held inside," Jackson said.

Gabriel nodded. He wanted that. At least when he got a chance—not *if* he got a chance—to talk to Marlena, it would be nice to have news of the Connelly family being okay to counter the utter heartbreak he knew she'd feel at her brother's betrayal.

He pulled off the last of the pieces of the lock and grabbed hold of the doorknob. Drawing a deep breath, he opened it, gun ready, and stepped inside.

Disappointment shuddered through him as he stared at what the bunker contained. Pot plants, rows and rows of marijuana plants, thriving beneath a ceiling full of brilliant grow lights.

"So Cory didn't want to leave here and get on with any life other than growing and selling weed," Andrew said, his voice filled with disgust.

"I'll let you all deal with this and hunt down John. I'm heading back to the hospital to check on Marlena." Now that Marlena's attacker had been arrested, and with no other place to look for the Connelly family, Gabriel's need to be at Marlena's side reared up in full force.

Half an hour later, Gabriel eased down in a chair next to Marlena's hospital bed. It seemed like a million hours ago that she had told him she loved him, that she'd offered up her love as a gift for him to carry with him wherever he went.

He stared at her still, lifeless face in the illumination from a light over the bed, and his heart ached for her. Upon Gabriel's arrival a few moments ago, he was told by the doctor that he felt certain she was going to be just fine, and it was only a matter of how long it would take her to slough off the effects of the drug she'd been given.

She was going to be fine. She'd wake up and wonder what had happened, and then he'd have to tell her about Cory. He'd watch her beautiful eyes fill with disbelief, then horror and then a sadness that would take his breath away.

He didn't want to tell her about Cory, but he refused to allow anyone else to break the news to her. She would need comfort, and he wanted to be the man who gave it to her. He was the only man he felt could give her what she needed.

He leaned his head back and closed his eyes. They'd managed to solve half of the crime. Marlena would no longer be in danger, but they'd still failed to find the Connelly family.

There would be nothing holding her to the bed-and-breakfast anymore. As soon as she was on her feet, she would leave alone to discover what life might hold for her, and he would remain here until his director pulled them off the case or sent them on another one.

The moment she drove away from the bed-and-breakfast, their lives would diverge, and he would do nothing to stop that from happening. He realized he cared about her deeply, and maybe it was possible that she did truly love him, but that only made it more important that he let her go.

He'd never learned to give or accept love, and Marlena deserved far more than he'd ever be capable of giving her. That must have been his last thought before drifting off to sleep, for when he opened his eyes the next time, the sun was shining bright, and he knew it was midmorning.

Marlena still slept, and so he slipped into the bathroom to clean up as best as he could. He washed his face, used a finger to brush his teeth and then raked his hands through his hair, trying to restore some sense of order.

When he stepped out of the bathroom, she remained in the same position in bed, but her eyes were open, and she looked at him in confusion. "Gabriel, I'm in the hospital."

"Yes, you are." He returned to his chair next to her.

She sat up, a hand raised to her head as if she were dizzy. "What happened?"

"First things first. How are you feeling?" he asked.

"A little groggy and a lot confused," she replied.

He leaned forward, hating what he was going to do to her, hating Cory even more for what he'd done to his sister. "What's the last thing you remember from last night?" he asked.

She dropped her hand from her head and frowned thoughtfully. "I remember talking to you." Her cheeks flared a becoming pink. "And then Cory came in. He brought me a glass of chocolate milk." Her frown deepened. "And I don't remember anything after that. What happened, and how did I get here?"

He reached out and drew one of her hands in his as her eyes grew wary. "You were drugged."

She stared at him as if he'd spoken gibberish. "Drugged? When? By whom?"

He held her gaze and squeezed her hand, and he saw the realization darken her eyes.

"No," she whispered as she tried to pull her hand from his.

He tightened his grip on her hand, not allowing her to draw away from him.

"There must be some mistake." Her voice was faint, and a tremble had begun in her.

"Cory drugged you, Marlena. He drugged you, and then he put cottonmouths in your bed."

She gasped, and tears shimmered on the length of her lashes.

"I came into your room to ask you a question, but you were unconscious, and the snakes were in bed with you."

Even though she shook her head no, he didn't stop, wasn't even sure he could stop if he wanted to. He needed to get it all out, one hard cut and then bandage it up as best he could.

"It was Cory who pushed you into the pond that night. It was Cory who shoved you down the stairs, and last night he drugged you and hoped that venomous snakes would kill you."

The tears that had barely clung to her eyelashes released, streaking down her cheeks. But he knew she believed him, knew he would have no reason to lie to her.

"Why?" she finally asked. "Why would he hate me so much?" She pulled her hand away, and this time he released hers as she began to cry in earnest. She hid her face with her hands, deep sobs wrenching through her.

Her pain was a visceral ache inside him, and his need to hold her, to comfort her, was too big for him to contain. For the first time in his life he felt the need to be close to another human being. He wanted a physical contact that had nothing to do with intimacy and everything to do with the desire to soothe.

Before it was even a thought in his head, he got out of his chair and got into the bed with her. She turned and sank into him as he wrapped her in his arms and held tight until the storm inside her had calmed.

Even after she'd stopped crying, he continued to hold her. Somewhere in the back of his mind he knew that, like the night they'd made love, a moment like this would never happen between them again.

"All I ever did was love him." The words were warm against his neck as she cuddled against him.

"I guess sometimes that isn't enough," Gabriel replied, and stroked her hair. "There is a core of rage inside him that I think might be tied to your mother's abandonment. He believes he doesn't need anyone."

He finally released her and returned to the chair. "He and John apparently had a plan for their future that they didn't want you to screw up by taking Cory away."

"A plan?" Even with her eyes reddened from her tears, she looked beautiful as the sunlight from the windows caught and sparkled on her blond curls.

"Did you know about the bunker where Daniella and Macy were held when Frank kidnapped them?" he asked.

"Daniella mentioned something about it, but nothing specific."

"I found it last night, and it's now filled with marijuana plants and grow lights. I can only assume that Cory and John have been in the business of selling dope for a while now."

Marlena closed her eyes and shook her head. When she looked at him again, her eyes were filled with a wealth of sadness but also a weary acceptance.

"I want to see him," she said.

"He's in jail, along with John." Jackson had texted

him at some point while Gabriel had slept to let him know that John had been pulled over in his car heading out of Bachelor Moon and was now residing in a cell next to his business partner.

"What's going to happen to him?" Her voice trembled from the depth of her emotions.

"He's facing a lot of charges. It will be a while before he even goes to trial, but I expect he'll do time in prison." He didn't try to soften it. He knew Marlena was strong and wouldn't want anything but the truth.

She sat up taller. "When can I get out of here?"

"The doctor has to release you. Are you ready to leave?"

"I feel sick to my stomach, my heart aches and my whole world has been turned upside down, but other than that I feel fine."

"Once the doctor releases you, then I'll take you to the jail to talk to Cory if that's what you feel you want to do," he offered.

She gazed at him for a long moment. "Actually, I'd rather go to the jail alone. You've done enough for me, Gabriel. You found out who was trying to hurt me, and you've removed the threat. You need to get back to your team and proceed with your investigation into the disappearance."

She looked down at her hands in her lap. "I appreciate everything you've done. You've saved my life twice, and I think if I feel up to it tomorrow, I'll pack up and be on my way. There's absolutely nothing left for me here."

It was a goodbye. Gabriel felt it in his heart, the sharp ache of absence that was about to begin. Wasn't that what he wanted? A sharp, clean break? A return to what had been his normal for so many years?

"Are you sure you don't want me with you when you go to see Cory?" he asked as he got up from the chair.

Her amazingly beautiful green eyes held his gaze. "Thanks, but I'll be fine alone." There was a new strength in her voice, a glint of steel in her eyes. She had spoken of her love of him, and he knew that now she was letting him go.

"How do you plan to get back to the bed-and-breakfast?" he asked.

"Don't worry. I'll figure it out," she assured him.

Gabriel took several steps toward the door. "Then I guess I'll see you back at the house."

"Just expect me when you see me," she replied.

He nodded and then left her room. He stood out in the hospital corridor and realized there was a part of him that wanted something more.

Then he shook his head, as if to dislodge the alien desire, and headed for the exit.

Chapter Fourteen

Marlena left the jail near dusk. It had taken forever to convince the doctor that she was fine and ready to be released. He'd insisted that she remain until after lunch, and then she'd realized she had nothing to wear home. She'd apparently been brought into the hospital in a nightgown, and nobody had thought to bring her any clothes.

A kind nurse had offered to loan her a spare set of scrubs, and so she'd finally left the hospital clad in a lavender short-sleeved scrub top, matching bottoms and a pair of flip-flops that had been in the lost and found.

It wouldn't have mattered if she'd been dressed in diamonds and pearls; nothing would have made her conversation with Cory any less difficult.

As she'd faced the young man she'd raised and loved, it had been like speaking to a stranger. He didn't even pretend to have any feelings for her other than hatred. He'd accused her of being the one who had driven their mother away, the one who had ruined his life. He'd told her over and over again that he would never love anyone, especially not her. He had nothing but hatred for her.

She'd left the sheriff's office around five and had sat on a bench just outside the building, trying to process everything that had happened, what had gone so terribly wrong.

She'd tried to be a mother to Cory. She'd sacrificed over and over again for him, not because she'd needed to but because she'd wanted to do whatever she could to keep him safe, healthy and happy.

Something was broken inside of him. She realized that now. Something had broken a long time ago that could never be repaired. She couldn't love him enough to fix him.

Twilight had begun to fall when Sheriff Thompson walked out of the building, obviously surprised to see her seated on the bench. He sank down beside her, his face wreathed with lines of age and weariness. "It's tough."

"It is," she replied. "I'm planning on leaving town tomorrow. Is that a problem with you?"

"Shouldn't be, although I'd appreciate an address for wherever you wind up, in case we need you when this all comes to trial."

She nodded, not wanting to think about a trial where she would have to stand and face Cory in a court of law.

"Cory confessed to trying to kill you, and both he and John have confessed to the pot field in the bunker, but both of them are adamant that they had nothing to do with the Connellys' disappearance," he said.

"Do you believe them?"

Thompson released a deep sigh. "I tend to believe them, but it's hard not to consider the possibility that Sam found out about the bunker, so John and Cory did what they had to do in order to save their illegal business."

"I might believe that if it wasn't for Macy. No matter how much Cory hated me, I can't imagine him doing anything to harm that little girl."

"And John maintains he had no idea what Cory was doing to you, that he's never committed a violent act against anyone in his entire life." Sheriff Thompson shrugged. "I suppose time will tell what really happened to the Connellys. Are you waiting for somebody to pick you up?"

"Actually, I'm not sure how I'm getting back to the bed-and-breakfast. I sent Gabriel home before I got out of the hospital."

"I'll take you home." He stood and hitched up his pants over his protruding belly.

"Thanks, I'll take you up on that." Together they headed for his patrol car parked in front of the office.

They drove for several minutes in silence. Finally it was the sheriff who spoke. "I should have retired after Daniella and Macy were kidnapped the first time. I've tried to help the Feds in any way I can, but I forgot about the bunker. Hell, the door was so well hidden Sam and I would have never discovered it if he hadn't followed Frank and found it. I never thought anyone would ever find it again. That was a huge mistake on my part." There was a wealth of regret in his voice.

"Don't blame yourself. There were things going on here that none of us saw."

Silence filled the car again for the remainder of the ride. As they drove into the parking area of the bed-and-breakfast, Marlena was surprised to see Gabriel sitting on the front porch, the shades of sunset painting him in orange and pink.

She thanked the sheriff for the ride, and as she got out of the car, Gabriel stood. As she came closer, she realized he'd been waiting for her. Two glasses of lemonade sat on the table, their ice cubes nearly melted. He must have been waiting for a while.

Sheriff Thompson waved to him and then pulled out of the drive as Marlena climbed up the porch steps and sank into a chair next to the one he had vacated.

He sat back down, and for a few minutes they remained there, watching the sun ease lower in the sky. "There's lemonade here if you're thirsty," he finally said.

"Thanks." She picked up the glass nearest her and leaned back in the chair. Numb. She felt a numbness sweeping over her. She hadn't fully processed what Gabriel had told her in the hospital about Cory until she'd come face-to-face with her brother behind bars.

She almost blessed the numbness that kept a wealth of sadness at bay. Tomorrow she would leave here without her brother. All the plans she'd made for him, for his future would never occur.

Funny, she'd never felt truly alone because she'd had Cory to care for, to love. And now there was nothing…nobody. For the first time in her entire life she was truly alone.

"Where did you get the clothes?" He frowned. "I didn't even think to bring you anything when I rushed back to the hospital last night."

"A nice nurse let me borrow these. I'll return them to her tomorrow on my way out of town."

"So you're still planning on taking off tomorrow?"

"There's nothing to keep me here." She took a sip of her lemonade and placed the glass back on the table.

"How did it go at the jail?"

She continued to stare at the sinking sun, not wanting to look at him, for a large part of her heart would remain here with him. "Awful. I always believed he was a good, well-adjusted kid. Oh, I knew he occasionally smoked pot. He thought I was too stupid to smell it on him, but I did. I just didn't see the darkness inside him, how much he hated me, how much he was afraid to love for fear of being let down again."

She stood, not wanting to spend another minute out here, where she could feel his concern for her wafting from him, where his scent rode the soft evening breeze.

She refused to sit out here and allow her love for him to lighten the darkness Cory had placed in her heart, to let Gabriel offer her support without love, caring without commitment.

"I have a lot of things I need to get done now so that I can take off tomorrow. I won't be cooking tonight, so you all are on your own."

"We'll be just fine," he assured her.

She picked up her glass and paused at the door, stupidly waiting for him to tell her not to leave, to get up and take her in his arms, to tell her he'd discovered he was in love with her.

"Maybe you and Cory have it right," she finally said dispiritedly.

"What do you mean?"

A wariness bounced into his eyes, and she knew he

probably didn't like to be compared to a person like her brother.

She shrugged. "Maybe it isn't good to love people because somehow, someway, they always let you down." She didn't wait for his response but hurried into the house.

She set her glass in the kitchen sink and then went into her private rooms, locking the door behind her. She sank down on the sofa and eyed the doorway to her bedroom.

Snakes. Cory had drugged her and then had put snakes in her bed. He'd tried to drown her in the pond and he'd pushed her down the stairs, all in efforts to kill her.

She hadn't realized that his hatred of her had begun when their mother had left and Marlena had taken over caring for him. He'd resented her, resented everything she'd done for him. She'd loved him, and he'd hated her.

It was definitely time for her to move on with her life, and this time she'd focus on working her way through school, getting her teaching degree and building a life for herself.

Alone.

Without love.

Because she wasn't sure she believed in love anymore. It was something that had brought her far more pain than it ever had pleasure. It had been a teenage girl's fantasy, and now she was a woman. It was time to put away foolish dreams.

"WHAT ARE YOU doing sitting out here in the dark?" Jackson asked as he stepped out on the front porch where Gabriel had remained long after Marlena had gone inside.

"Just sitting," he replied, glad that his voice didn't sound odd around the huge lump lodged in the back of his throat.

"Want to talk about it?" Jackson sat down next to him.

"Not really." Gabriel's stomach had been tied in knots since Marlena had left the porch.

"Andrew rustled up some soup and sandwiches for dinner. It's on the table."

"Thanks, but I'm not hungry. In fact, I think I'm going to head into town and have a couple of beers." It was the last thing on his mind, but he felt the need to escape, to run, and now with his decision made, he got up from the chair and pulled the car keys from his pocket.

"Are you going to be late?"

"No, Mom. I shouldn't be too late," Gabriel said sarcastically.

"Hope it helps," Jackson said as he got up from the chair. As he went inside, Gabriel headed for the car, his thoughts and emotions in turmoil.

He intentionally tried to keep his mind blank as he headed to the Rusty Nail Tavern in town, but thoughts skittered like wind-tossed leaves inside his head, with no direction or focus.

They still had no clues as to what had happened to the Connelly family. When he'd learned of the existence of that bunker, he'd wished that they would be in there safe and sound.

No clues, no direction in which to take the investigation and now no Marlena. He tightened his hands on the steering wheel. He didn't want to think about her. Tomorrow she would be on her way, and he and his team would remain at the bed-and-breakfast until they were told to leave.

He pulled into the parking lot of the tavern, grateful it was early enough that there wasn't much of a crowd. Once inside he found a stool at the end of the counter and ordered a beer.

As he nursed the drink, he thought about everything that had happened. Cory had been a shock. He couldn't imagine the depth of masked anger that had built up to a point where he'd tried to kill Marlena not once but three times.

What bothered Gabriel more than anything was that, while Cory was screaming to him that he hated Marlena, that he would never love anyone but himself, Gabriel had seen a tiny piece of himself in the young man.

Like Cory, Gabriel had internalized his mother's abandonment to mean that love had no place in his life. Like Marlena's troubled brother, Gabriel had chosen to turn his back on love, to live his life alone without loving or being loved.

But Marlena loves you, a little voice whispered inside him. She'd dug in, seen the good inside his soul and fallen in love with him.

What he found far more disturbing than anything that had occurred over the past couple of days was her parting words before she'd gone into the house.

Somehow this entire experience had made her believe that she was wrong about love, that her belief in love was stupid. And that broke Gabriel's heart.

He felt as if somehow he and the circumstances had destroyed something beautiful inside her, and that sent a searing pain through him.

By the time he'd finished his second beer, he realized coming here was a mistake. There was no amount of beer in the world that would set things right.

It was time for him to wrap his mind back around the Connelly case and nothing else. He'd come to Bachelor Moon to find a missing family, not to fall in love, and it was time he got back to doing what he did best.

He left the tavern feeling no more settled than he had when he'd arrived. It was just after nine when he returned to the bed-and-breakfast, and Jackson and Andrew were seated on one of the sofas in the common room in front of the television.

"Back in one piece," Andrew said as Gabriel sprawled in a nearby chair.

"Yeah, I had a couple of beers and decided it was time to come home." He forced a grin at Jackson. "I didn't want to stay out so late that I got grounded."

Jackson returned his smile and then sobered. "So where do we go from here on the Connelly case?"

"I don't know," Gabriel admitted with frustration. He glanced toward the kitchen area. "Has Marlena been out of her rooms?"

"No. When I was making dinner, I heard her moving around. I assumed she was packing things up to take off tomorrow," Andrew replied.

Gabriel stood. "I think I'll head on to bed. We'll sit down in the morning and figure out our plan of attack on this case."

As he climbed the stairs to the lavender bedroom,

he thought of how beautiful Marlena had looked in the lavender scrubs. Even after a night of being drugged, without makeup and beaten up by life, she'd looked stunning.

She'd looked like a woman he'd want to see every morning, like a woman he'd want to hold every night before falling asleep. He shucked his clothes and got into bed, willing himself to sleep so he wouldn't have to think anymore.

He awoke at dawn, and after a long, hot shower he headed down the stairs, where the scent of coffee indicated that Marlena was up.

He poured a cup of the fresh brew and sat at the dining room table. He could hear her moving around in the kitchen, apparently preparing to fix breakfast. Other than the soft rattle of dishes, there was no other sound.

No soft, sweet humming to start the day. Apparently that had even been stolen from her by the events that had happened. *You stole it from her,* a little voice screamed inside his head. *You stole her music, her joy of life...you and Cory.*

Within minutes he was joined at the table by Jackson and Andrew, and the talk turned to the Connelly case and what their possible next steps might be.

Marlena entered the room, carrying with her a platter of waffles and another of sausage patties. Gabriel barely noticed the food. Instead he drank in her loveliness. But as he looked closer, he noted that her eyes were dark, sad and haunting.

"I'll be right back with the syrup," she said and left the room. She returned only a moment later with a large jug and set it in the center of the table.

"This will be the last meal that I'll fix. After I clean up the breakfast dishes, I'll be on my way."

"Where are you headed?" Andrew asked, his plate already filled with the food she'd delivered.

"I'm thinking New Orleans."

Gabriel couldn't help but notice that her gaze had refused to meet his.

"You'll like New Orleans," Jackson said. "It's my favorite place to party in the entire state."

She smiled at him, and Gabriel found himself jealous that her smile wasn't directed at him. "I'm not looking for a party. I'm just looking for a life."

"I wish you all the happiness in the world," Andrew said around a mouthful of waffles.

She smiled at him fondly. "And I wish you and your almost fiancée happiness, and I hope you never have to eat a convenience-store sandwich again."

She returned to the kitchen, and Gabriel felt the emptiness inside him. He had to cast her out of his head. He grabbed two waffles and smothered them with syrup, as if the food on his plate could fill the emptiness in his heart.

He ate without enthusiasm, not tasting anything, and afterward he went upstairs to his room to retrieve his laptop. He lingered in his room, not wanting to hang around downstairs while she cleaned up the dishes.

When he finally returned to the dining room, she'd disappeared into her quarters, and Jackson and Andrew awaited him at the dining room table to discuss their investigation.

Just as Marlena walked out of the room with two suitcases in her hands, Jackson's phone rang. He held up a hand to halt any conversation and listened to whoever was on the other end of the phone. "Yes, sir. Yes, I've got it. I'll tell the others."

He disconnected and placed his phone on the table. "That was Director Miller. We're being pulled out of here."

"Why?" It was Marlena who spoke. "Sam and Daniella and Macy are still missing." She dropped her suitcases to the floor.

"What's going on?" Andrew asked.

Jackson frowned. "You two are being sent back to the office in Baton Rouge and I'm heading to the Kansas City office to work a new case. An FBI profiler and her sheriff husband have vanished into thin air from a small town called Mystic Lake."

"So this may be bigger than the Connelly family," Andrew replied.

Jackson nodded. "I'm going to see if what they're dealing with there is what we have here."

"I called Pamela last night and told her I was leaving today, so she could move in here or whatever." Marlena's eyes held a new sadness. "If you all aren't going to be here, then I can't imagine what's going to happen to this place."

She leaned down and picked up her suitcases, then looked at Jackson. "Find out what's going on, Jackson. You might be the only one with access to some of the clues that will lead back to Sam, Daniella and Macy."

He nodded. "I'm going to do my best. I guess we need to head upstairs and pack." Together he and Andrew headed for the stairs, leaving Gabriel and Marlena alone.

He'd noticed as he'd come down from upstairs that she'd already parked her car in the lot out front. He reached out and took one of her suitcases from her. "Come on. I'll walk you out."

HER FOOTSTEPS FELT heavy, even though she knew she should be happy to be finally moving on. She'd hoped that when she left Bachelor Moon, Cory would be in her passenger seat and that Sam, Daniella and Macy would be standing on the porch to wave goodbye.

As devastating as Cory's betrayal had been, her stupidity over loving Gabriel was almost as hard to deal with. He'd warned her, and she hadn't heeded his warnings. He'd told her to pretend that their night together had only been a dream, but it was the one piece of reality she wanted to take with her.

They reached her car, and she opened the trunk. She put her suitcase in and then moved aside so he could do the same with the one he carried.

Instead of placing it in the trunk, he dropped it to the ground. "We need to talk," he said.

"There's nothing left to say. Two bad guys are in jail, three people are still missing and you're going back to Baton Rouge while I'm heading to New Orleans." She didn't want to talk any more with him. It hurt too much. Even standing here in the midmorning sunshine and looking at him created a deep ache inside her.

"I can't let you leave here disillusioned and no longer believing in love," he said, his eyes a dark, troubled blue.

"I think I've told you before that, even though you're

a big bad FBI agent, you don't get to tell me how to think or what to feel."

"But it's important to me that you believe in love." He took a step closer to her, too close.

Why was he torturing her? Why didn't he just throw the suitcase into the trunk and let her go? Why on earth did he suddenly want to talk about love?

"I don't know why what I believe is important to you now," she replied.

He took yet another step toward her, bringing with him that scent that had always made her feel safe and secure. She wanted to run away from him. She also wanted to run into his arms. Instead she stood frozen in place until he moved so close to her that she could feel his body heat.

"It's important to me that you believe in love, because you've made me believe in it. You've made me believe I'm worthy of being loved, of taking a chance and giving a special woman my heart."

A lump rose in the back of her throat and tears began to burn behind her eyes. "Then I hope you find that special woman." She was grateful her voice didn't crack, that she didn't dissolve into tears. She should be happy that she'd been able to do that for him, that he would go into his future with an open heart.

"I've already found her," he said softly. He raised a hand to touch one of her curls, and then swept his hand down the side of her face in a caress.

Her heart stopped beating and then began to bang rapidly at his words. He dropped his hand from her face and instead streaked a hand through his own hair.

Stepping from one foot to the other, he looked decidedly uncomfortable.

"I'm not very good at this," he confessed, as if she didn't know him well enough to figure that out, but she had no intention of making it easier on him, despite the fact that her heart was on the verge of soaring.

"You're going to have to do a lot better than that," she replied. "Right now you're just a dream that I was supposed to forget."

"Marlena, without you I'm a man only half-alive." His eyes were the blue of truth. "I'm in love with you. I fought against it. I didn't want it." He looked down at the ground and then back at her. "I was definitely afraid to give my heart to anyone. I saw a little part of myself in Cory, and it scared the hell out of me."

"You could never do what Cory did," she replied, the thought of her brother churning up her heartbreak where he was concerned.

"True, but I was well on my way to being a lonely, bitter man, and then I came here and met you. You made me believe in love, and I don't want you to go to New Orleans. I want you to come with me to Baton Rouge. I love you, and I don't want to spend a single day without you in my life."

"Are you going to keep talking or are you going to kiss me?" she finally said.

His eyes turned the deep blue that always made her heart soar. He pulled her into his arms and lowered his mouth to hers. His kiss spoke all the words he might not have said and more. It tasted of love, of desire and of a sweet commitment she'd never expected to find.

As somebody cleared his voice, Gabriel broke the

kiss. Andrew and Jackson stood nearby, their duffel bags in their hands, obviously ready to leave Bachelor Moon behind and get on with new assignments.

"What's up?" Jackson asked.

Gabriel didn't break his gaze with Marlena. "Is it a yes?"

"Is this a dream that I have to forget later?"

His gaze softened. "No, this is a reality I want to live for the rest of my life. You and me together—that's the reality I want."

"Oh, Gabriel, I want that, too."

He finally stopped staring at her to look at his partners. He reached into his pocket, pulled out the car keys and threw them to Jackson. "You two go ahead. Marlena and I will head out in her car in a few minutes."

"Looks like something good came out of our time here," Andrew said, looking first at Gabriel and then at Marlena, his face wearing a broad smile. "In fact, it looks like something great happened."

Gabriel reached for Marlena's hand, and she came willingly to his side. "I found a new partner, and I think it's going to be one of those forever partnerships."

"I know it will be," she replied with conviction and squeezed his hand. Some of her joy tempered as she gazed at Jackson. "I hope you find something in your investigation in Mystic Lake that will lead to answers about the Connellys."

"That's the plan," he replied. "And now we're heading out. Marlena, I expect I'll be seeing a lot of you when I get back from this new assignment."

"And thanks for everything you did for us to make our time here as pleasant as possible," Andrew added.

She smiled at Andrew. "Go home and put a ring on Suzi's finger. Life is too short to waste a minute."

A moment later she and Gabriel watched as the car with the two agents pulled out of sight. She turned back to the man she loved. "Are you sure this isn't a wonderful dream?"

"I'm sure." He pulled her back into his arms. "You are the woman I want by my side until the day I die. I want to hear you humming in our kitchen. I want to see that beautiful smile every morning. I want your love surrounding me, as I intend to surround you with all the love I kept bottled up inside me for so many years."

Once again his lips claimed hers, taking her breath away. She was leaving Bachelor Moon with the heartbreak of her brother's betrayal, with unanswered questions about the missing people she loved, but she'd also leave with the man she knew would fulfill her dream of love forever.

He might have needed a special woman to awaken his capacity to love, but he was the special man she'd wanted, the man who would be her best friend, her lover and eventually her husband.

She would embark on her new life not alone but with Gabriel, the man she knew would make all her dreams of love and family come true.

* * * * *

#1461 JUSTICE IS COMING
The Marshals of Maverick County
by Delores Fossen
Marshal Declan O'Malley is stunned when he's confronted by Eden Gray, P.I.—and by the immediate attraction between them.

#1462 YULETIDE PROTECTOR
The Precinct: Task Force
by Julie Miller
A detective's icy heart may be the casualty when a stalker threatens to silence his star witness.

#1463 COLD CASE AT CAMDEN CROSSING
by Rita Herron
Sheriff Chaz Camden must keep Tawny-Lynn Boulder alive long enough to find out what happened to his sister.

#1464 DIRTY LITTLE SECRETS
The Delancey Dynasty
by Mallory Kane
While investigating a senator's murder, Detective Ethan Delancey and eyewitness Laney Montgomery are thrust into a world of blackmail and lies.

#1465 THE CRADLE CONSPIRACY
by Robin Perini
A woman found with amnesia turns to a man who battles his own PTSD to save a missing baby.

#1466 UNDERCOVER TWIN
by Lena Diaz
A drug-enforcement agent must work with his ex-girlfriend to save her twin sister and bring down a drug lord.

———————

YOU CAN FIND MORE INFORMATION ON UPCOMING HARLEQUIN® TITLES, FREE EXCERPTS AND MORE AT WWW.HARLEQUIN.COM.

REQUEST YOUR FREE BOOKS!
2 FREE NOVELS PLUS 2 FREE GIFTS!

⬧ HARLEQUIN®

INTRIGUE®

BREATHTAKING ROMANTIC SUSPENSE

YES! Please send me 2 FREE Harlequin Intrigue® novels and my 2 FREE gifts (gifts are worth about $10). After receiving them, if I don't wish to receive any more books, I can return the shipping statement marked "cancel." If I don't cancel, I will receive 6 brand-new novels every month and be billed just $4.74 per book in the U.S. or $5.24 per book in Canada. That's a savings of at least 14% off the cover price! It's quite a bargain! Shipping and handling is just 50¢ per book in the U.S. and 75¢ per book in Canada.* I understand that accepting the 2 free books and gifts places me under no obligation to buy anything. I can always return a shipment and cancel at any time. Even if I never buy another book, the two free books and gifts are mine to keep forever.

182/382 HDN F42N

Name _____ (PLEASE PRINT)

Address _____ Apt. #

City _____ State/Prov. _____ Zip/Postal Code

Signature (if under 18, a parent or guardian must sign)

Mail to the **Harlequin® Reader Service:**
IN U.S.A.: P.O. Box 1867, Buffalo, NY 14240-1867
IN CANADA: P.O. Box 609, Fort Erie, Ontario L2A 5X3
**Are you a subscriber to Harlequin Intrigue books
and want to receive the larger-print edition?
Call 1-800-873-8635 or visit www.ReaderService.com.**

* Terms and prices subject to change without notice. Prices do not include applicable taxes. Sales tax applicable in N.Y. Canadian residents will be charged applicable taxes. Offer not valid in Quebec. This offer is limited to one order per household. Not valid for current subscribers to Harlequin Intrigue books. All orders subject to credit approval. Credit or debit balances in a customer's account(s) may be offset by any other outstanding balance owed by or to the customer. Please allow 4 to 6 weeks for delivery. Offer available while quantities last.

Your Privacy—The Harlequin® Reader Service is committed to protecting your privacy. Our Privacy Policy is available online at www.ReaderService.com or upon request from the Harlequin Reader Service.

We make a portion of our mailing list available to reputable third parties that offer products we believe may interest you. If you prefer that we not exchange your name with third parties, or if you wish to clarify or modify your communication preferences, please visit us at www.ReaderService.com/consumerschoice or write to us at Harlequin Reader Service Preference Service, P.O. Box 9062, Buffalo, NY 14269. Include your complete name and address.

HII3R

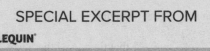
"I've watched you for the past two days, so I knew you take a ride this time of morning before you go into work."

"You watched me?"

She nodded.

"Are you going to make me arrest you, or do you plan to keep going with that explanation?"

"I'm a P.I. now. I own a small agency in San Antonio."

She'd skipped right over the most important detail of her brief bio. "Your father's Zander Gray, a lowlife, swindling scum. I arrested him about three years ago for attempting to murder a witness who was going to testify against him, and he was doing hard time before he escaped."

And this was suddenly becoming a whole lot clearer.

"He sent you here," Declan accused.

"No," she quickly answered. "But my father might have been the reason they contacted me in the first place," Eden explained. "They might have thought I'd do anything to get back at you for arresting him. I won't."

He made a sound of disagreement. "Since you're trespassing

and have been stalking me, convince me otherwise that you're not here to avenge your father."

"I'm not." Not a whisper that time. And there was some fire in those two little words. "But someone's trying to set me up."

Declan thought about that a second. "Lady, if you wanted me to investigate that, you didn't have to follow me or come to my ranch. My office is on Main Street in town."

Another head shake. "They didn't hire me to go to your office."

"So, who are they?"

"I honestly don't know." She dodged his gaze, tried to turn away, but he took hold of her again to force her to face him. "After I realized someone had planted that false info on my computer, I got a call from a man using a prepaid cell phone. I didn't recognize his voice. He said if I went to the cops or the marshals, he'd release the info on my computer, that I'd be arrested."

"This unknown male caller is the one who put the camera outside?"

"I think so."

He shook his head. "If they sent you to watch me, why use a camera?"

"Because the camera is to watch *me*," she clarified. "To make sure I do what he ordered me to do."

"And what exactly are you supposed to do?" Declan demanded.

Eden Gray shoved her hand over her Glock. "I'm to kill you."

Will Eden and Declan be able to work together, or will their past get in the way?

Don't miss the edge-of-your-seat action in
JUSTICE IS COMING
by USA TODAY bestselling author Delores Fossen.
Available November 19, only from Harlequin Intrigue.

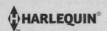

INTRIGUE

THREATS INSTEAD OF CHRISTMAS CARDS

As the lone surviving victim who can put her attacker away in prison, heiress Bailey Austin becomes the key to the D.A.'s case against a notorious criminal. As lead detective, Spencer Montgomery must prep her for trial. But he becomes her personal protector when she starts receiving terrifying "gifts" meant to scare her away from testifying. Her courage touches him in ways no other woman has, and reminds him that she's more important to him than any investigation.

YULETIDE PROTECTOR

BY *USA TODAY*
BESTSELLING AUTHOR

JULIE MILLER

Available November 19, only from Harlequin® Intrigue®.

HI69729

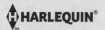

INTRIGUE®

THE OLD SAYING IS TRUE: THE SMALLER THE TOWN, THE BIGGER THE SECRETS

People in town believe Tawny-Lynn Boulder is the reason the Camden Cross case went unsolved. She survived the bus accident that left several dead and two missing, but the severe trauma left her with amnesia. When she returns seven years later, Sheriff Chaz Camden reopens the case and asks for her help. But someone in town keeps threatening to kill Tawny-Lynn to keep the case closed. Now she must trust the sexy sheriff for protection. Together, they'll show this murderer that in Camden, accidents don't happen…justice does.

COLD CASE AT CAMDEN CROSSING

BY RITA HERRON

Available November 19, only from Harlequin® Intrigue®.

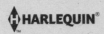